PENGUIN BOOKS

# Buddy

NIGEL HINTON was born in London in 1941, during an air raid. He worked in advertising and as a teacher before becoming a full-time writer. He is the author of the Beaver Towers series for younger readers as well as three books about Buddy for teenage readers. He is married and lives in East Sussex.

**www.nigelhinton.net**

*Books by Nigel Hinton*

BUDDY

TIME BOMB

# Nigel Hinton
# Buddy

PENGUIN BOOKS

PENGUIN BOOKS

UK | USA | Canada | Ireland | Australia
India | New Zealand | South Africa

www.penguin.co.uk
www.puffin.co.uk
www.ladybird.co.uk

Penguin Books is part of the Penguin Random House group of companies
whose addresses can be found at global.penguinrandomhouse.com.

Penguin
Random House
UK

First published by J. M. Dent & Sons Ltd 1982
Published in Puffin Books 1984
Published in this edition 2016
001

Text copyright © Nigel Hinton, 1982
Words from 'Everyday' by Norman Petty and Charles Hardin used by permission
of Southern Music Publishing Co. Ltd, London

The moral right of the author has been asserted

Set in 12.2/18 pt Dante MT Std
Typeset by Jouve (UK) Milton Keynes
Printed in Great Britain by Clays Ltd, St Ives plc

A CIP catalogue record for this book is available from the British Library

ISBN: 978-0-141-36895-5

All correspondence to:
Penguin Books
Penguin Random House Children's
80 Strand, London WC2R 0RL

*For Peter Prince*

# Chapter One

Buddy stole the money from his mother's purse just before he left for school. His mother was in the kitchen clearing up the breakfast things and his father was still in bed.

He tiptoed into the front room and slipped the purse out of her handbag. He clicked it open and took out a £5 note. A wave of disgust swept through him. Only two weeks ago he'd vowed to himself that he was going to stop shoplifting and here he was stealing from his own mother. He hadn't done that since he was a little kid and had sometimes nicked the odd ten pence. He was turning into a real thief. There must be something the matter with him. First, the shoplifting. He'd done it a couple of times with some other boys from school. They had stopped but he'd gone on doing it alone. And now, this.

He heard his mum come out of the kitchen and, in a moment of panic, he fumbled with the catch on the purse. It wouldn't close properly so he just chucked it back in the bag still open. He put the handbag back on the sofa, crumpled the note into his pocket, and went out of the room. His mum was in the hall putting on her coat.

'Hurry up, you're late,' she said and then called up the stairs. 'Terry!'

There was no answer from his dad. His mum called out again and then started up the stairs.

Buddy put on his shoes and while he was tying up the laces he heard angry voices coming from upstairs. Another row. Recently, there'd been more rows than anything else. He hated to hear his mum and dad shouting like that.

'I'm going,' he called. There was no reply so he went out of the front door, slamming it behind him.

The morning at school was terrible. The money for the class trip didn't have to be handed in until lunchtime so he knew he could still change his mind. He went through the arguments again and again. He could take the money back. His mum was bound to have noticed it had gone – money was precious since the factory had closed and his dad had lost his job. He could always leave it lying on the floor, as if it had fallen out of her bag.

He didn't even want to go on the trip – £4 to see some stupid castle and safari park. On the other hand, he didn't want to stay behind again. It would be the third thing he'd missed this term alone. The other times – the visit to the

2

theatre and the trip to the Three Counties Agricultural Show – he'd been the only one not going from 3E. He'd had to join another class for the day and it had been awful.

This time he hadn't even bothered to ask for the money. He knew what his parents would say: 'We can't afford it.' Well, it was all right for them. They still had the things they wanted. They both smoked; that cost a fortune nowadays and it was bad for them. And his dad had started going out to the pub in the evenings. His mum moaned about that, saying it was a waste of money and he was mixing with the wrong crowd again, but it didn't stop him doing it.

The more Buddy thought about it, the more it seemed that he had right on his side. If his mum and dad had to give up smoking and drinking for a couple of days – so much the better. It would be good for them.

Still, he hesitated a moment when Mr Normington said, 'Right, 3E, hands up the people who brought the money for the trip to Newton Castle.' Buddy looked round and saw everybody's hand go up. Then he raised his, too.

His dad was out when Buddy got home and his mum wouldn't be back from work for nearly an hour. He went to his room and got on with his homework. He was just finishing some French when the front door banged.

'Buddy!'

His heart lurched. His mother's voice sounded sharp and angry. He heard her running up the stairs. Then his door opened.

'Where is it?' she asked.

'What?'

'Don't play innocent with me – the £5 you took from my purse this morning.'

Buddy denied it a couple of times. He even suggested that perhaps it had been stolen by someone at her office. Then, suddenly, he couldn't hold out any longer. He admitted he'd done it and started to explain why.

He'd expected her to be furious but what happened was worse. She began to cry. She leaned against the wall and tears ran down her face. He stood, shocked and ashamed for a moment, then moved towards her. He wanted to hold her, to beg forgiveness.

'I'm sorry,' he mumbled and reached out to touch her, but she pushed him away.

He tried again but this time her temper broke and she shouted, 'Get away. Leave me alone. You're as bad as him. Like father, like son – that's what you are!'

Buddy backed away and sat on the bed. His mum stayed there, crying, for a few minutes then she wiped her face roughly and went to the door. She didn't look back but

Buddy heard the one word she said, quietly but full of bitterness, 'Thief!' She went out of the room and closed the door.

He lay on the bed and cried. She had looked so pale, so hurt. The lines near the mouth, the dark rings around her eyes – he had caused those. Once or twice he tried to defend himself in his own mind but each time he remembered her face and her tears and the way she'd said 'Thief'. Perhaps she even knew about the shoplifting.

After about an hour he undressed and got into bed. He wasn't hungry and he couldn't bear the idea of going down and facing his mum. Not long after, she came up and opened the door. He closed his eyes tight, pretending to be asleep. She said his name once but he didn't move and she went away.

He lay there for ages, thinking. If only there was some way he could turn back the clock to this morning. If only he'd never taken the money. 'Like father, like son.' He knew what she meant: the big secret; the thing they never talked about. It had happened four years ago when Buddy had been nine. For three months his dad had disappeared. His mum had just said that he was away somewhere for his work, but Buddy had missed him terribly and the atmosphere in the house had been tense and gloomy. Then, when his dad came back he'd taken Buddy for a walk and told him the truth – just suddenly in the middle of the park.

'I've been in prison,' he had said, 'three months for breaking and entering. But it's all over, see. I've done time and that's it. We'll forget it, OK?' Then, after a long pause, 'Still love me?'

Buddy had nodded and his dad had given him a hug.

And now – now his mum thought it was going to happen to him, too.

Some time, much later, he woke up. There was an argument going on downstairs. It must be about him. His mum must have told his dad and now they were shouting at each other because of him. He put the pillow over his head and pressed his ears to keep the sound out.

The next morning, the house was very quiet. He got dressed and went downstairs. His dad was asleep at the kitchen table with his head resting on his arms. Buddy shook him and he sat up.

'Where's Mum?' Buddy asked, the blood pounding in his ears.

'Gone.'

For one terrible moment Buddy felt as if he were going to laugh.

'Where?'

His dad shook his head.

For the rest of that day, Buddy was certain she'd be home when he got back from school – but she wasn't. Then he gave it a week. She'd be back within a week.

His dad cooked the meals and they ate them in silence. They did everything in silence. Buddy ached to talk about it – to say he was sorry – but he couldn't. The only thing his dad said was not to talk about it to anyone – not at school, nowhere. Buddy promised and it made him feel more hopeful. His dad must want to keep it quiet because he thought she'd be back soon.

The week passed. Then another, and another. Gradually, as it turned into months, Buddy gave up hope. She wasn't coming back. And it was all his fault.

# Chapter Two

Buddy left his house at eight o'clock. He didn't have enough money for the bus so he'd have to walk. If he could get to school without stepping on a single crack in the pavement everything would be OK. Not everything – that would be too much to ask. What then? He wouldn't get into trouble for wearing jeans. He'd get a good mark in the Biology test. And he wouldn't die until he was old. How old? Over sixty. Right. But no cheating. All the way, and not a single crack.

By the time he reached the High Street he was fed up with the effort of watching every step. The jeans and the test didn't matter but he couldn't give up now because of the other thing. If he broke the bargain he might die at any time. Today. Tomorrow. It happened to people of his age – even younger. There was that girl in junior school – she'd got some blood thing. She went into hospital and never came out. Then there was that boy in Year Eight – he'd been knocked off his bike by a lorry. There'd been rumours that his head had been squashed flat.

He went on, stepping carefully, trying to plant his feet firmly in the middle of every paving stone. Stupid to set himself mad tasks like this. Perhaps he was mad.

Anyway, what was dying? Everybody had to die some time. But what was it like? Could you look down and see yourself lying there dead? Brendan Jonson once told him that if you died in your sleep it was like being asleep for ever, but that if you died in an accident or someone murdered you it was like being murdered or run over for ever. As soon as he heard it, Buddy knew it was the sort of idea that would keep floating in and out of his mind. And it did – nearly every day.

All kinds of crazy things came into his brain nowadays. Stupid thoughts like his name had a curse on it. Buddy Holly – his dad's favourite singer – had died at twenty-two and now he would die young because he'd been named after him. And stupid games: if he held his breath until a bird flew off a wire his mum would be at home when he got back after school. Then cheating and making a loud noise to scare the bird because he couldn't hold his breath any longer.

If people could see a quarter of the weird things in his head they'd lock him up in a loony bin like a shot. Like now: people were giving him strange looks because of the

9

way he was having to walk to avoid the lines. They already had their suspicions. Buddy Clark the loony – he even walks differently.

As if he didn't look different enough already. Blazer, miles too short at the sleeves. Jeans, instead of grey trousers. Shirt, not nearly as clean as his mum used to make them. And a stinking white plastic bag to carry his books and things. More than anything he hated that. Everybody else had smart satchels or even – the latest trend in his class – businessmen's document cases, hard and heavy and very useful for smashing into other people's shins on the stairs.

Sometimes he almost wished he'd never been promoted to the E stream. E for Express. The top stream. The stream that would take exams early. E for Exams.

He'd been so thrilled at the end of Year Seven when his class teacher had told him he was going up because his tests had been excellent. E for Excellent. It had seemed like the best thing that had ever happened to him. It would have been except – E for Except – he wasn't like the others.

It wasn't just that they all seemed to be able to buy whatever they wanted. It was the way they talked. The things they talked about. The way they casually used names – names of newspapers and books, names of places they'd been to, names of things their parents had bought.

They weren't cleverer than he was – in fact some of them were not as clever – but they were different.

It was the difference between hard, black document cases and a white plastic bag. It was arriving at school on your bike or in your parents' car – not walking up the street trying not to step on lines on the pavement.

Buddy took two more careful steps and turned with relief on to the tarmac of the school drive. He'd done it. His legs ached from the strain but not once had he touched a line.

It didn't do him any good, of course. As soon as he started up the stairs to his classroom he felt a tap on his shoulder. It was Mr Normington, 3E's class tutor.

'I told you about those yesterday,' Mr Normington said, pointing at his jeans. 'You said it was only while your mother was repairing your trousers.'

'Yes, sir.'

'Well?'

'She hasn't done them yet,' Buddy said, taking care with the 'h' of 'hasn't'.

'Why not?'

For a moment Buddy wanted to tell him, wanted to shout, 'Because I haven't seen her for five months – that's why.' That would soon shut him up.

'I don't know, sir.'

Mr Normington sighed. 'It's always you, isn't it? Letting down the standards of the rest of the class.'

Mr Normington was always talking about standards. He'd been in the school before it had been reorganized. Standards had been so much higher then. The Express classes had to maintain those standards. The Express classes were the last bastion, not just of academic standards but of dress and behaviour, too. 'Bastion' was one of Mr Normington's favourite words.

He put his hand on the back of Buddy's neck and squeezed – not hard enough to complain about, but hard enough to show that he could hurt him if he wanted to.

'Upstairs. And no denim tomorrow.' Squeeze, squeeze. Push, push. Up the stairs and into the classroom.

Buddy sat down at his desk near the door and noticed that Julius and Charmian weren't in their places behind him. He hoped the twins weren't away. He'd never had black friends before – in fact, he'd said some nasty things to some black kids at his junior school. But he'd been drawn to Julius and Charmian because they were the only other people who didn't fit in with the rest of the class. He'd started off by admiring the cheerful way they ignored all the spiteful jibes that the other pupils, and even some of the teachers, made. They'd become his allies and then, gradually, his closest friends.

Mr Normington started calling the register. He looked up when there was no answer from Julius and Charmian. 'The Rybeero twins still away?' There was a little smirk on his face as he added, 'I wonder where our ace students can be?'

He put a heavy emphasis on the word 'ace' and everyone knew what he meant. Yesterday they had been learning about similes and someone had suggested 'As black as the ace of spades' and he'd said, 'That's certainly a simile but I don't think Master and Miss Rybeero would approve if they were here!'

People had sniggered then and they were sniggering now.

Buddy wanted to say something to wipe the silly grins off their faces. Wanted to tell them that they were stupid snobs and that the twins were better than all of them put together.

At the very least he could have sat stony-faced as his friends were mocked. But he smiled. Mr Normington was looking in his direction and, in an attempt to show that he belonged in 3E, and that he was on the side of Mr Normington's bastions and standards, Buddy smiled and joined in the general chuckle.

He hated himself for wanting to belong to all that, but it was true – he did. A huge part of him wanted it.

The rest of the day went badly and he was almost glad. It was a punishment for betraying his friends. Two more teachers told him off about his jeans and he got less than half marks in the Biology test. So much for the stupid pavement game. He was still going to die young.

At afternoon registration Mr Normington handed out forms about the parents' consultation evening later that month. Buddy was so busy brooding about the idea of his dad coming to school that he only half listened as Mr Normington went on about the litter in the classroom.

'Well, who's responsible?' Mr Normington barked in his loudest voice.

Buddy looked up and just happened to catch the teacher's eyes on him.

'It weren't me, sir,' he said and then cursed himself for the mistake.

'Wasn't. It wasn't me,' Mr Normington sneered. 'Well, frankly, I don't care. Since you speak and look like a dustman, you can do a dustman's job. Clear it up.'

There was absolute silence in the room as he went round the desks picking up the bits of paper. He didn't look at anyone. A couple of people near the back slyly put their feet on the pieces, making it harder to pick them up. His hands were dirty when he finished.

As he threw the paper into the bin he vowed that one day he would get his revenge.

# Chapter Three

When Buddy got home from school he saw his dad standing outside the house. He was in his shirtsleeves and he was arguing with a man. The man was raising the tailboard of a truck. His dad's Harley-Davidson was on the truck. Buddy could hear his dad swearing.

The man finished locking the tailboard then walked round and got into the cab. His dad followed and banged on the door. There was a puff of blue smoke from the exhaust of the truck as the engine started. His dad kicked the front tyre. The man inside tooted the horn. His dad stood back and the truck drove away.

Buddy hid behind a hedge so that his dad wouldn't see him. When he peeped out a minute later, the street was empty. It didn't look like his house without the Harley-Davidson outside. That motorbike was his dad's most important possession. He'd be heartbroken – or angry. Or both.

Buddy opened the back door quietly. The kitchen smelled of stale frying which always clung to his clothes. He'd been aware of it ever since one of the boys in his class had pushed him away, saying 'Ugh, you stink like a fish and chip shop, Clark.' After that he'd told his dad that he didn't want a fried breakfast any more. His dad had seemed almost hurt.

'You need something hot in you,' he'd said. 'Nothing like it – egg and fried slice first thing.'

But Buddy had insisted he'd rather have cereals. Since then he'd had breakfast alone – in the front room. His dad stayed in bed now, as if cooking Buddy's breakfast had been the only reason for getting up.

He went along the hall and opened the door of the front room. His dad was slumped on the sofa, his eyes closed. He'd kicked his shoes off and there was a big hole in one of his bright green socks. When Buddy had been a little kid he'd got lost in a big shop. He'd sat on the floor and cried until he saw his dad coming. On the floor, in the middle of all those legs, he'd known it was his dad because of the socks. Nobody else's dad wore green or pink fluorescent socks.

'Dad,' he said.

There was no answer. He walked over to the window and looked out. There was a patch of oil on the little bit of concrete outside. His dad had put the concrete down so that his bike would have somewhere to stand. He'd taken down the fence and laid the concrete over the tiny strip of grass that had been the garden. The council had sent a man round to complain but his dad had just laughed. Buddy had to admit it looked a bit ugly, especially now the bike had gone. Perhaps the grass would grow up through the concrete.

There was a loud sigh and the plastic material on the sofa squeaked as his dad moved. In the old days, when things had been fun, his dad used to make them all laugh about the rude noises the sofa made when someone moved on it.

There was a long silence and Buddy could almost feel the pressure of it in his ears. Then, suddenly, his dad spoke. 'Pigs. They've took me 'arley.'

Taken – my – Harley. Buddy clenched his teeth to stop himself correcting his dad. That happened all the time now. He was so used to being corrected at school that it was almost a habit. His dad had threatened to knock his block off if he kept doing it, but that wasn't why he'd tried to stop. It was that look in his dad's eyes – a look that said, 'Are you ashamed of me?' And the awful truth was that he was, sometimes. And his dad knew it.

'I nearly done the bloke over. Told 'im I'd get the money. Only owe a couple of months. It's always money.'

There was a thump as his dad hit something. Buddy knew he shouldn't have come in here – not with his dad in a mood like this. He knew what was coming next. He wanted to get out but he couldn't move; he felt too awkward.

'I s'pose you need some tomorrow and all.'

Buddy dug his fingernails into his palms. It wasn't fair. He couldn't help it if he needed money sometimes. Why did his dad always start on about it?

''Ere, you. I'm talking to you.'

'Nothing.'

'What?'

'I said "nothing". I don't want any money.'

'Blimey, that makes a change. Supposed to be free, schools. Don't make me laugh. If they was free, I'd still 'ave me 'arley.'

Suddenly all the events of the day crashed in on him and he turned round boiling with anger. 'I haven't even got proper trousers. My others are all worn out.'

'They wouldn't be if you took proper care of them,' his dad snapped back.

'I did take proper care of them. They're worn out. And they're too small. I've grown. What do you expect me to do – stop growing?'

'Don't you get cheeky with me. You're asking for trouble, you are.'

'Yeah? Well I have to wear jeans and I get into trouble for that.'

'Tough luck.'

'And it's tough luck about your Harley. It's not my fault. If you had a flipping job . . .' Buddy stopped. He was trembling. Tears of rage had filled his eyes. He blinked and they rolled down his face.

His dad stood up and for a moment Buddy thought he was going to come across and hit him. Instead, he just glared, then turned away. Buddy grabbed his plastic bag and ran out of the room, slamming the door. He thought of slamming out of the front door, too, but he couldn't think where to go. He tiptoed quietly up to his bedroom.

He lay down on his bed. He shouldn't have said that about the job. All right, but what about the things his dad had said: he didn't take care of his trousers. They were two years old. They were too tight and too short. There were holes in the inside leg because they'd worn too thin. Like his dad's socks – they had holes in them. He wished he'd said that. He never thought of clever things like that until it was too late.

He still shouldn't have said that about the job. He should have stayed calm and not got into an argument about that. Whatever else he was, his dad wasn't lazy. He'd tried and tried for jobs since the factory had closed. Buddy knew that. Jobs were hard to find.

It was cold in the bedroom but he didn't move, didn't even bother to get into his sleeping bag. Shadows filled the room as it got darker. He lay and gazed out of the window. The house next door blocked most of the view but he could see a triangle of dark blue night sky. There was one bright star in the triangle. He closed his eyes and wished.

When his dad called up the stairs and asked if he'd like something to drink, half of him wanted to say yes. He wanted the argument to be over, to be able to go down and sit and drink a cup of tea with his dad. The other half wanted something more – wanted to stay up here in the cold, alone. It wanted to hurt his dad, make him pay for the things he'd said, make him miserable.

'Buddy? Do you want some tea?' his dad called again.

'No,' he shouted, trying to make his voice sound sad.

'Cutting off your nose to spite your face' – that's what his mum always used to say about moods like that. Well, he'd just cut off his nose.

Ten minutes later there was the sound of music from down below. It was loud – one of his dad's records. He strained to hear which one it was. All those old 45s and the precious 78s that he wouldn't let anyone touch; they were much more than music to his dad. They were memories, dreams, hopes. And, sometimes they were messages.

Buddy knew all the voices, all the names. He'd learned the songs like nursery rhymes when he was a kid. This one was a woman. Brenda Lee. 'Little Miss Dynamite' his dad always called her. The song was 'I'm Sorry'.

The record ended and a minute later Buddy heard his dad leave the house.

# Chapter Four

Buddy didn't get warm all evening. He'd become really cold while he'd been lying on the bed but he didn't allow himself to put his fan heater on – it was too expensive. He made himself a piece of toast and a cup of coffee then went back to his room and lay on the floor to do his homework. By the time he finished writing, his whole front was almost numb from the cold lino.

He sat on the bed and wrapped his sleeping bag round himself while he read a book and made notes for his History special study. The teacher had made them each choose one famous person to find out about and give a short speech on to the rest of the class. It was Buddy's turn tomorrow.

He had chosen Richard the Lionheart because he'd seen a good film about him. The film had made him seem like a great hero but the more Buddy read, the less he liked him. He seemed to spend most of his life killing people just because they weren't Christians. Some hero. His death was horrible, though. He got hit in the neck by an arrow. Someone cut the arrow out, but the wound went rotten and he developed gangrene.

Buddy didn't want to read about it but he couldn't stop. Richard took days to die, and he knew he was dying and he kept talking about it. What had he really felt, though? Had he been scared? He'd been forty-two when he died. Only two years older than Buddy's dad.

He closed the book and looked at his watch. Ten thirty. Where was his dad? He'd been out nearly four hours. He felt a surge of panic. Supposing something had happened – an accident. He tried to take his mind off the thought by getting himself ready for bed. He straightened the sleeping bag – no sheets and blankets since his mum had left – and went to the bathroom.

He washed his hands and face and looked at himself in the mirror. He was pale, and the dark hair above his lip seemed darker than ever. His mum always said he'd had a moustache even as a baby. He ran his hand over his cropped hair – he liked the way it felt, spiky but soft. His dad hated it, though, and said he looked like a convict.

Ten forty. Where was he? Terrible thoughts flew through his head. Hospitals. Ambulances. Nurses drawing curtains. A doctor coming out and speaking quietly to him, 'I'm sorry to have to tell you this . . .' Would they make him identify the body?

The front door slammed and he dropped his toothbrush in shock.

'Buddy?'

'Dad.' He rushed down the stairs, his face breaking into a grin of relief. The house suddenly seemed warmer and lighter.

'Get some plates,' his dad said, holding up a brown paper bag.

'What?'

'Plates, cloth-ears. And knives and forks. I've got some Chinese for us.'

Buddy got everything and went into the front room. Music was playing and the little cartons of Chinese food were all open on the floor. His dad served the food, making corny jokes about Flied Lice and Sweet and Sour Eyeballs.

As soon as he started eating, Buddy realized how hungry he'd been. How miserable and worried, too. Now, everything was different. His dad was singing along to the music between mouthfuls, and the row of the afternoon was forgotten.

'Met an old mate of mine tonight,' his dad said as he finished eating, and rolled himself a cigarette. 'Might do a bit of work for him.'

'Honest? That's great. What is it?'

'Oh, you know – this and that. See how it turns out.'

'What is it? Sort of like factory work?'

'It's work – all right? It ain't even certain yet.' There was a snappy edge to his voice that stopped Buddy asking any more questions.

He washed up the plates, made a cup of tea for his dad and then went up to bed. He felt warm and sleepy after the food, and he was already dozing off when he heard the door open.

'You asleep?'

'Nearly – not yet.' Buddy sat up. His dad was standing in the doorway. His face was in shadow.

There was a long silence, then his dad said, 'We do all right – don't we? You and me?'

'Course we do.'

'Yeah, well . . .' He took a couple of steps into the room and then turned as if he was about to go out again.

'I'm glad about the job.' He wanted his dad to stay. 'I got all worried tonight.'

'What about?'

'I don't know – stupid things. I thought something might have happened. Accident or something.'

'Won't get rid of me as easy as that,' his dad said, and laughed.

There was another silence and Buddy longed to go on talking about it. He counted to three and forced himself to say it. 'Do you think about it – dying and all that?'

'Yeah, sometimes. Happens, don't it.'

'What do you reckon it's like?' His voice cracked with the embarrassment of saying it out loud.

'Dunno. Can't be worse than this, though, can it?'

His dad wasn't trying to help at all but now he'd started, Buddy was determined to go on. 'I keep thinking about it. I didn't used to.'

That was true – he never used to worry about it before. It had happened just after his mum left. His dad had spent ages listening to a record called 'Endless Sleep' about a girl who drowned in the sea. He'd suddenly got frightened about his dad dying and it hadn't stopped there. For the first time ever, he'd realized that one day he, Buddy Clark, was going to die. He'd said it and thought about it before, of course, but he'd never really believed it. This time, he'd known it was true and it had been like falling off a cliff – except he never got to the ground and he was still falling.

It was the sort of thing he could've talked about with his mum. She'd have listened and then told him she understood and not to worry, it was only a phase he was going through. That's what she always said about things that worried him – 'It's only a phase . . .' But she wasn't there now and he needed his dad to say it.

'You been watching too many 'orror films on the telly,' his dad laughed. ''Ere, I 'eard a story tonight that'll give you the shivers. About this 'ouse in Croxley Street.'

'What, Croxley Street – here in town?' Buddy didn't want to hear any story that would give him the shivers, but he wanted his dad to stay.

'Yeah. Number 56. Supposed to be haunted. Some geezer cut his wife's throat with a knife about twenty-five years ago and then strung 'imself up. They reckon 'er ghost walks round the rooms all covered with blood. Now nobody wants to live there.'

'Don't blame them,' Buddy said.

'Nah, some people'd believe anything.'

'Don't you believe in ghosts?'

'Once you're dead, you're dead.'

Buddy couldn't think of anything to say. He wished he'd never started it in the first place. He just hoped he wouldn't dream about 56 Croxley Street.

'Oh well, better turn in,' his dad said.

Buddy wanted to tell him to leave the door open but he knew what a joke his dad would make of that. The door closed and the room was in darkness. He wriggled down as far as he could into his sleeping bag and tried to think of other things. What would Mr Normington say when he turned up in jeans again? Would he be able to do his History speech OK? He tried to remember the main points of what he was going to say but he kept imagining the arrow in Richard's neck.

Stop it.

He made himself think of his mum. He tried to picture her face. It was difficult – he could only catch glimpses of it. Surely he couldn't have forgotten what she looked like already? At last he caught a full picture of her in his mind. Holding it there, he fell asleep.

# Chapter Five

The next day went well. For a start, Mr Normington was away ill and none of the other teachers said anything about his jeans. Secondly, it was Friday: Buddy's favourite day – a good combination of lessons and the weekend to look forward to. Best of all, Julius and Charmian were back – though they still had sniffly colds and Julius moaned that their mum always made them go back to school before they were completely better.

The History speech went really well, too. It was the last lesson of the day and he grew more and more nervous about it as it got nearer the time. Then, as soon as he started talking he relaxed and found he had a lot to say. Mr Grey said it was an excellent speech and Buddy sat down feeling great. The only sour note came at the end of the lesson. Everybody was leaving the room and Charmian patted him on the back and said, 'Well done – terrific speech.'

David Siddell, who was just ahead of them, turned round and sneered, 'Yeah, not bad for a dustman, was it?'

A couple of other people laughed and shouted, 'Dustman!' then Siddell started singing,

> 'My old Buddy's a dustman
> He wears a dustman's hat
> He wears gorblimey trousers
> And he lives in a council flat.'

Buddy made a grab at him but Siddell ducked away and ran down the corridor and began singing again. Buddy started to run after him but stopped as Siddell dashed out of the main door and away.

'Just ignore him,' Julius called.

'What's he on about anyway?' Charmian asked.

Buddy told them about the incident with Mr Normington and the litter. They crossed the playground and went through the gates on to the street.

'I hate that place,' Buddy said, looking back at the school.

'Forget it – it's Friday,' Charmian said.

He waited at the bus stop for the twins' bus and arranged to meet them later at the Satellite. As the bus drew away, he crossed the road and started to walk home. There was no hurry so he went the long way through the shopping precinct. When he got to Lawrence's, the big department store, he looked at the windows and then went in.

Another game. This time it was the 'I can walk through here without nicking anything' game. He strolled through the stationery department. He'd nicked a couple of pens from here at the beginning of the year. So stupid, all that risk and worry for a couple of cheap ballpoints. Well, he'd learned his lesson. He'd never do it again.

He stopped in front of the pen counter and picked up a ballpoint that wrote in three different colours. He flicked the colour selector and scribbled on the little notepad that was there for testing the pens. It was a good pen. He looked round – nobody near. He checked the ceiling – were there any TV cameras? It would be so easy to slip the pen into his pocket. He put the pen back in the display and walked on.

There, he'd done it. He'd passed the test – he could resist the temptation. He walked out of the swing doors and could barely stop himself from smiling. Just imagine if he'd taken the pen; a store detective might now be tapping him on the shoulder and asking him to go up to the manager's office. The police would be called and they'd take him down to the police station. They'd ask questions – questions about everything. They might even find out about his dad's prison record. He could just see their reactions. They'd shake their heads and say, 'Goes to show – runs in the family. Like father, like son.'

Well, they were wrong. He'd just proved it, hadn't he? He could've nicked the pen but he hadn't. He'd learned his lesson.

His dad was out so Buddy had his tea on his own. There wasn't a lot to choose from so he toasted a slice of bread and heated up a small tin of peas. It made a change from beans on toast but he was still quite hungry when he finished. He read for a while then went up to his room. He wasn't sure what to wear. His parka was really too small and he couldn't get it on if he wore more than a shirt underneath. In the end he decided it'd be warmer to wear two sweaters instead.

The Satellite Youth Club was held in a dingy hall next to the church where the twins went every Sunday. Buddy enjoyed going, though he still felt a bit awkward about being one of the few whites among so many blacks. There was always a worrying moment as he went in, when he would look round anxiously to check that Julius and Charmian were there. He'd hate to be there on his own so he usually turned up late to make sure.

He pushed open the door and caught sight of Charmian at once. She was in the middle of the floor, dancing with a couple of other girls. Julius was over by the side door talking with a tall, thin boy who was wearing a floppy, purple corduroy cap and a long, black overcoat. Buddy walked round the dance area and joined them. Julius slapped him on the shoulder and said 'Hi', but the other boy stared at him then pulled his cap down nearly over his eyes.

'This is Buddy,' Julius said, but the boy turned away. Julius looked at Buddy and raised his eyebrows.

'I'm going to play table tennis,' Buddy said quickly and walked towards the far end of the room. He could see that the tables were full but he kept going in order to get away from the difficult situation with Julius's friend. What was it all about? The boy's eyes had been filled with hatred.

He watched the people playing table tennis for a bit then glanced back down the hall. Julius was still talking with the boy and Charmian was still dancing. He wished he could pluck up courage to go and dance – Charmian was with Marcia and Estelle and he knew they would be friendly. He needed a welcome after the coldness from the tall boy but he hated dancing, especially since the girls danced so well.

He looked at the three of them, rocking to the rhythm of the record that boomed from the speakers. They moved together, doing complicated steps, their whole bodies in harmony with each other and the music. Once, one of them made a false step and they all stopped for a moment. Then as they got back into the pattern of steps again, they

33

grinned with pleasure. White, white teeth against the black skin. Buddy found himself grinning with them.

Charmian saw him and waved. It was strange how she could always make him feel happier. Since his mum had gone she was almost the only one he could speak to. Not about everything, of course. She knew his mum had gone – he'd told her even though his dad had said he mustn't tell anyone. Charmian had promised not to say a word. Buddy wasn't bothered about that anyway. He couldn't really understand why his dad was so anxious to hide it – loads of marriages broke up. What Buddy didn't want people to know was why she'd gone. He'd almost blurted it out to Charmian one day but at the last moment he'd felt too ashamed.

Buddy watched the girls dancing for a bit longer, then someone called him over to play doubles at table tennis. It was a long, closely-fought match and when he and his partner won they were immediately challenged by another pair. The second match was just as long and tense and quite a number of people came over to watch. Buddy glimpsed Julius but he was too caught up in the match to notice if the tall boy was still with him. Buddy felt good and he played well.

'Hey, you play OK,' Julius said, coming up to him at the end.

Buddy shrugged but he felt like smiling. 'Where's that other bloke?'

'Oh, Dennis – he's gone. Don't mind him – he had a bit of bother from some white kids at his school today.'

'So did I,' Buddy said.

'Yeah – yeah, I should've told him that. Not the same, though.'

'Why not?'

'Just isn't,' Julius said vaguely and then groaned. 'Oh no – it's the minister. Must be nearly time to finish. Let's get Charmian. I want to get out before he starts.'

Julius clattered over a couple of chairs and dashed on to the dance area. Buddy had to laugh. Julius went through things, not around them, and he always moved at a mad speed. Charmian was only half an hour older but, looking at them now, you'd never guess they were twins: Julius was jumping around and waving his arms like a kid while Charmian, taller and smiling gently, tried to calm him down.

'OK, Jules,' Charmian was saying as Buddy walked up, 'just don't make it obvious. Come on, Buddy, we've got to sneak out – Jules thinks he's too cool for prayers.'

They moved casually around the side of the hall until they were near the exit. They watched the minister hold up his hands as a signal that the club was closing. The record was switched off and everyone stopped. The minister walked to the middle of the hall and, as he turned his back, Julius whispered, 'Now!' They slipped out through the door, followed by a couple of other people. Julius laughed in triumph.

'You wait,' Charmian said, 'I bet he noticed – he'll say something about it on Sunday.'

'Who cares – he shouldn't do prayers at the club, it's not a church,' Julius said and then began imitating the minister. 'Brethren, don't let us forget to thank the Lord for our pleasure this evening. Thank Him for the music . . .' He did it so well that even Charmian had to laugh. 'Thank Him for the electricity. Thank Him for the floorboards.' Julius went on saying even madder things until they got a fit of giggles that lasted all the way to the fish and chip shop.

Buddy said he wasn't hungry and he waited outside while the twins went in. Actually, he was starving and he moved away from the tempting smell coming out on the warm blast of air. It was quite cold out now and the inside of the window was all misted over. Somebody was drawing on the steamy glass – a picture of a woman with enormous breasts. Buddy peered through the lines into the shop and saw Julius' grinning face.

'What did you think of my picture of Charmian?' Julius asked as they came out of the shop.

'Shut up, Jules – I don't look like that,' Charmian said, looking down at herself.

'You do, doesn't she, Buddy?'

'I do not. Take it back or you don't get any chips.'

'OK, you're as flat as a pancake,' Julius said, holding out his hand.

Charmian unwrapped the paper, took out a bag of chips and handed it to her brother. Then she held out another bag for Buddy. He took a chip but Charmian said, 'Not one – the bag. They're yours.'

'I said I never wanted any,' Buddy said, feeling a blush of embarrassment creep up his neck.

'Well, I bought some anyway.'

'You'll just have to take 'em back, won't you?' He felt stupid as soon as he said it and walked away to cover it up. He walked fast and he heard the twins almost running to keep up.

Suddenly Charmian grabbed him and swung him round. She looked him straight in the eye and said, 'Please. I don't want you to pay for them.'

That was worse. She knew he had no money. Stubborn pride wouldn't let him accept them. 'I don't want them.'

He started walking again, then Charmian ran past with Julius after her. She stopped next to a lamp post and held the three bags of chips over a litter bin.

Julius turned, 'Stop her!'

'I'll do it,' Charmian said and tipped the bags slightly. A couple of chips fell out.

'She'll do it, Buddy. She's got mine, too.'

'It's all eat or no one eats,' Charmian said and tipped the bags some more.

'Stop her,' Julius shouted.

'OK, I'll eat them,' Buddy said. 'Just for Jules.'

Charmian smiled and handed him a bag. Julius grabbed his bag and started gobbling his chips as fast as possible. 'You're mad, Char – really mad,' he mumbled with his mouth full.

'Don't eat and speak at the same time, Jules,' she said in a joky voice.

They stopped when they got to the Astoria and looked at the posters and photos outside. There was a film on called *Night of Dracula*. Julius put two chips in his mouth and let them hang out like fangs.

'I don't know why they're always X films – we saw one on TV, didn't we, Char? And it wasn't scary at all.'

'Some bits were.'

'No, it was dumb. I like monsters better than all that ghosts and vampire stuff.'

Buddy started telling them what his dad had said about the haunted house. He even made up a few gory details to make it sound more interesting. As he finished the story the wind blew bitingly cold along the street and he shivered.

'Cor, that's great,' Julius said, jumping with excitement. 'They ought to make a film about that. Hey, let's go and look at it.'

'No, it's a waste of time,' Buddy said.

But there was no stopping Julius. 'Oh, come on. Croxley Street's on the way back to our place. We can have a look at the house then you can come and have a cup of coffee with us.'

They set off down Malham Road in the direction of Croxley Street but while Julius and Charmian were talking and laughing excitedly, Buddy grew more and more uneasy. For a start, he didn't like the idea of seeing a house where a murder had taken place; but it was more than that. For no good reason he suddenly felt he shouldn't have mentioned the house.

# Chapter Six

The Germayne Arms stood on the corner of Croxley Street and the main road. The pub was bright and noisy and there were a lot of cars parked on the forecourt. Twenty yards further up Croxley Street, however, the light and the sound of laughter and music were left behind. The night closed in and only a few street lamps cast their circles of light in the darkness of the long road ahead.

The houses were tall and set back from the pavement, some with front gardens so large that there were trees in the middle of the lawns. The number of the house next to the pub had been 154; now they were passing number 82. Buddy calculated quickly – another thirteen houses to go. Thirteen – unlucky. Another warning. He moved to the edge of the pavement and tried to count the houses but he couldn't see that far.

'Let's cross over so we can see which one it is,' he said and the twins followed him to the other side of the road.

Even Julius had stopped chattering – perhaps he was feeling scared, too. The only sounds were their footsteps and the rustling of the trees in the wind. This must be the quietest street in town, and the darkest.

Buddy lost count of the numbers but it didn't matter because, when they reached it, it was obvious which one was number 56.

Tall, brick gateposts guarded the two entrances to the semicircular drive but there was only one gate and that was half open and hanging off its hinges. The other entrance looked like a barricade – with wooden posts and tangles of barbed wire. There was a tall, straggly hedge that hid the garden and the lower part of the house but what Buddy could see made the skin crawl on the back of his neck. The windows were all boarded up as if what was inside was too terrible to see, or as if someone had tried to stop something horrible from getting out.

'It's horrible,' Charmian whispered. 'Look at those turrets along the roof – it's like a castle.'

'Dracula's castle, my dear,' Julius hissed, and he pretended to bite her neck.

'Shut up, Jules – I don't like it,' she said, pushing him away.

'Doesn't scare me – it's only an old house. I'm going to have a look.'

Julius stepped off the pavement and walked across the road. He turned and waved to them, then slipped into the gap between the gate and the gatepost. He took a couple of paces up the drive and stood casually with his hands on his hips. Then he turned round and shouted, 'See? – Nothing.'

Suddenly he raised his arms and let out a long ghost-like howl. He ran out of sight behind the hedge and the noise stopped. There was a long silence, then Julius's grinning face appeared behind the posts and barbed wire of the other entrance. He waved and called, 'Scared you!'

He disappeared again behind the hedge and then strolled out of the gate and back across the road, looking very pleased with himself. 'Your turn, Buddy,' he said.

Buddy had known that Julius would dare him to go and he'd made up his mind to say no, but at the last minute he changed his mind. Julius was right: it was only an old house, even if some people had died there. So what – people must have died in almost every old house in town; that didn't make them scary. It was just an ordinary old house and he had to prove it to himself – if not he'd go on being scared by stupid things like ghosts.

'OK,' he said, and started crossing the road.

'Go up to the front door,' Julius called.

'OK.'

Yes, he would. He'd go right up to the front door. There was nothing to be afraid of. He had to stop acting like a kid. He was nearly fourteen, after all. It was ridiculous, all this stuff about ghosts and death. He had to stop it. If he walked up to the front door and stood there while he counted ten – no, twenty – it would be like a victory and all his fears would stop for ever.

He slipped between the gate and the gatepost. Something cold brushed against the back of his neck and he jumped. Just a twig from the hedge – it was nothing. He must keep going. His feet scrunched noisily on the gravel of the drive and he stopped. He looked back. He was hidden from the road. All he had to do was wait here for a bit then go back and tell them he'd done it. Besides, he was trespassing. Perhaps he'd be caught and reported to the police. Better to go back and stay out of trouble. No, he had to do it. If he cheated, everything would go wrong.

He stepped sideways on to the long grass of the lawn. No need to make any noise. Why not? There was nobody inside. It was just an old, empty house. Except that inside there a man had stabbed his wife and then killed himself.

He crossed the lawn and walked softly across the gravel up to the front-door steps. The steps were worn in the middle from all the people who had climbed them, including *them* – the man and his wife. Buddy got to the top step and looked at the front door. There was an old door knocker in the middle and on either side of it two planks had been nailed lengthways, presumably to cover glass panels. Halfway down was a large letterbox. He was just going to push it open and look through when there was a noise behind him. He whirled round and saw Julius and Charmian at the bottom of the steps.

'You scared me, you idiots. What're you doing?'

'Coming to look,' Julius said in a loud voice.

'Ssh! I'm going to look through the letterbox.'

As Buddy turned back to the door, Julius skipped up the steps and banged on the knocker. 'Anyone in?' he shouted.

Buddy ran down the steps and on to the lawn. Charmian ran with him and when they stopped, she called out, 'Come on, Jules, stop being stupid.'

Julius took no notice. He banged again then peeped through the letterbox. 'There you are . . . nothing. Come and see.'

Buddy and Charmian waited a moment then moved forward. As they climbed the steps, Julius suddenly straightened up and burst past them, almost knocking Charmian flying. She grabbed hold of Buddy and shouted, 'Julius, stop mucking about!'

They watched as he ran down the drive and out of the gate.

'Idiot,' Charmian said angrily and stooped to look through the letterbox. Buddy bent down just as she pushed open the flap. Through the large slit they saw a flickering candle and a white face staring at them.

Charmian screamed and together they flew down the steps in terror. Dashing across the gravel, Charmian tripped over the edge of the lawn. She crashed against Buddy and they both fell on to the wet grass. They stumbled up and ran blindly towards the gate. Buddy banged his elbow as he squeezed through, and a half-sob, half-laugh shook him. His legs felt weak with the pain and the panic but he forced himself to run. Charmian could hardly keep up with him but he grabbed her hand and pulled her after him. Ahead of them, Buddy could see Julius appear and disappear each time he ran through a pool of light under the lamps.

They didn't stop until they reached the warm brightness of the Germayne Arms. Julius was already there, leaning against a car on the forecourt, breathing harshly and coughing.

They walked quickly, keeping to the brightly lit main road instead of taking the darker short cuts. They were still out of breath and nobody spoke. Buddy's lungs felt raw and his elbow ached from where he'd banged it.

'Did you see it?' Julius panted at last. Now that they had their breath back, they all started talking at once. The strange thing was that they had all noticed different things. For Julius it had been the hand holding the candle – a hand that seemed to float by itself in the darkness. Charmian had seen a face, so pale that it had looked like a skull. While for Buddy it was the eyes he remembered – dark, liquid eyes sunk deep in the whiteness of the face. They had stared at him without blinking – the only movement had been the dancing reflection of the candle's flame.

## Chapter Seven

The twins' parents had converted the front room of their house into the office of Rybeero Taxis. There was a large desk, a couple of telephones and a small shortwave radio set. When Buddy followed the twins in through the door, Mrs Rybeero was at the desk speaking into the microphone. The speaker was crackling with the replies of the drivers, one of the phones was off the hook and the other was ringing. Mrs Rybeero waved to them and pointed to the phone.

Charmian picked it up and said, 'Good evening – Rybeero Taxis. Can you hold the line a moment, please?' She put the receiver down in front of her mother and then led the way through into the back room.

Buddy always liked this room. It was clean and neat but very cosy – the way his house had been before his mum left. There was a small kitchen area off the main room and they went in there to make some coffee. Now that it was all over and they were safe, they could laugh about how scared they'd been at the house. Julius kept trying to make it seem as weird and mysterious as possible by talking about ghosts, but Buddy and Charmian were certain that they had seen a human being.

'Ghosts don't bend down to peep through letterboxes, Jules,' Charmian said. 'And anyway, I saw his face. It was a man – I know it.'

'All right, if it wasn't a ghost who was it? Buddy said nobody lived there.'

That started them off guessing who the person could have been. Again, Julius made crazy suggestions about murderers or kidnappers but Charmian said it had probably been a tramp or someone like that. Buddy wasn't sure. He didn't agree with Julius's mad ideas but he couldn't help thinking that it was a bit more of a mystery than Charmian would admit. After all, the house was supposed to be empty and there was that story about it being haunted. And those eyes – although they had been human, they hadn't been ordinary. They had been sad and . . . what? . . . not normal.

When Mrs Rybeero came into the room twenty minutes later, Charmian stopped talking about 56 Croxley Street and pretended to be talking about the Satellite. She needn't have bothered because Mrs Rybeero had barely got through the door before she launched into a long description of the difficult evening she'd had. Buddy was always amazed to hear her talk because although the twins spoke exactly like all the other kids at school, their mother still had a strong Jamaican accent that was quite hard to understand.

'Ah swear ah going pull them phones off the line one day,' she finished, collapsing on to the sofa between Charmian and Julius and giving them a hug. 'You late back. Is wha you all been doing, eh?'

Charmian lowered her eyes and said, 'Oh, nothing. Is Dad out driving?'

'What you think?' sighed Mrs Rybeero. 'Him love the car more than me. Ah too fat for him now, eh Buddy?'

The sudden question caught him off guard and he said, 'Yes.' There was a moment of confusion in his mind as he tried to remember the question and then he tried to correct himself – 'I mean, no . . . I . . .'

But no one was listening. Mrs Rybeero was slapping her knee and roaring with laughter, and the twins were doubled up.

'Honestly, I didn't mean . . .' Buddy began again but it only made them laugh more. Mrs Rybeero now started patting her large stomach that was already wobbling with laughter. This was too much for Julius who rolled off the sofa on to his knees and started pounding the floor with his fists. Even Buddy's embarrassment faded and he joined in.

'Oooh my,' said Mrs Rybeero at last, still chuckling and wiping her eyes, 'you say the truth, child. "Out of the mouths of babes and sucklings" – yes, indeed. Now see they, them phones again – they fit for drive me mad.'

'I'll go,' Julius said.

'No, no – if you daddy hear you on the radio, he'll want to know why me didn't pack you off to bed an hour ago. You can bring a cup of coffee an' a couple a sweet biscuit. Then,' she added, giving them both another hug, 'the two a you, straight to bed.'

She heaved herself off the sofa. As she passed Buddy she patted her stomach again and gave him a huge grin.

Buddy went into the kitchen with the twins and leaned against the draining board while Charmian made the coffee and Julius opened a big tin of biscuits. Buddy noticed how clean and tidy the kitchen was and he thought of how dirty his was nowadays. Why couldn't his dad keep the house clean?

Julius took the coffee and the biscuits to his mum and Charmian put the things away and wiped the table where she'd spilled some sugar. Watching her, Buddy's moment of anger at his father suddenly seemed so unfair. After all, how often did he help by doing little things like that? Right, tomorrow he'd make an effort. He'd sweep and clean everywhere until their house looked as good as this one.

'I like your mum,' he said when Charmian had finished the table.

'Yeah, she's all right,' Charmian said, 'except she's always making us go to bed too early.'

'Yeah, my mum does, too.' It was a silly lie and Buddy looked at the floor. He was so used to lying that he'd forgotten that Charmian knew the truth.

To his complete surprise, she leant over and kissed his cheek. He was so startled that he didn't know what to do. His hand started to go to his cheek but he scratched his chin instead. He didn't want her to think he hadn't liked it and was wiping it away.

A door banged and Julius came through from the office. 'She says we've got to go to bed now,' he groaned.

'I'm just going anyway,' Buddy said.

'What are we going to do about it – you know, the house and everything?' Julius asked.

'Nothing. What can we do? It's all just . . . stupid, anyway.' Buddy suddenly felt depressed. The thought of going home, the lies he told, the things inside him – they all made mucking about around an old house seem childish.

Julius started to argue, saying it was good fun, but Charmian broke in, saying, 'Buddy's right. It's got nothing to do with us.'

'Blimey – first interesting thing in years and you . . .' sneered Julius, '. . . you're like a couple of old women.' He pushed a chair hard up against the table and went out. Buddy and Charmian laughed as they heard him stomp upstairs. There was a moment's awkward silence.

'Well, I suppose I'd better go to bed,' Charmian said.

'Yeah,' Buddy said. 'See you.'

He felt that he'd said it too quickly but there was nothing he could do now except go. He walked across the lounge and opened the door without looking back.

'Goodnight, Buddy,' Mrs Rybeero called as he went into the office. 'You catching bus?'

'No, I'll walk.'

'Outside cold. You going to catch you death without a coat. You want me call me husband? He can give you lift.'

'No, it's OK, honest. Does he work all the time?'

'Too much, child. Can't get drivers at all. He suppose to operate all this,' she waved her hand at the radio and the phones, 'but he was out so much. So if you know any drivers, you tell them 'bout us. What you dad do?'

'Oh, things – you know,' Buddy mumbled and started moving to the door.

'You mum work, too?'

'Yes. Goodnight, Mrs Rybeero,' he said quickly and went out of the door.

It was cold outside and the wind cut through his sweaters. He pulled the sleeves down over his hands and walked fast to keep warm. There were a lot of cars racing along the main road but the pavements were empty. A police car drew up at some traffic lights as he was crossing the road. The policemen inside looked at him and he tried to act casual. His heart beat fast. He stopped and pretended to look in a shop window as if he hadn't a care in the world. Then he thought that they might think he was planning to break in and steal something so he hurried on. He heard the car rev up behind him as the lights changed. The car passed him slowly but, although one of the policemen stared at him, it didn't stop.

Crazy, feeling like that. He hadn't done anything wrong. Not today, anyway. Yet he still felt nervous even when the car had disappeared from view. He knew it was just a mad fear but ever since that couple of weeks when he'd shoplifted nearly every day he'd been worried that the police knew or would find out about him. His heart tightened whenever he thought about surveillance cameras in shops. Perhaps they had photographs of him and were just waiting for the moment to arrest him. Perhaps he'd be stopped, out of the blue, like tonight, just to be asked what he was doing walking alone at night and one of the policemen would recognize him.

Mad. Loads of kids at the school nicked things all the time and they never got caught. Besides, that was all over – he was never going to do it again and if he hadn't been arrested yet, he was probably safe.

His house was dark when he got back. His dad must still be out. He checked upstairs but his dad's bed was empty and there were clothes dropped all over the floor. His mum used to complain that he and his dad always left their clothes lying about everywhere. He picked up the clothes and folded them on a chair.

The walk home had chilled him right through and it took him ages to get warm in bed. He'd left the landing light on and the door open but he still felt rather scared alone in the house. There were creaking noises that sounded just like someone coming up the stairs.

He covered his ears and thought back over the evening. Not the house and those eyes . . . He wouldn't think about that. Mrs Rybeero – she was fun. And she'd said they'd needed drivers. Perhaps his dad could get a job with them. Julius was a laugh. And Charmian . . . she was . . .

He woke with a start. There was someone on the stairs. He held his breath and listened. The bathroom light went on and there was the sound of running water. It must be his dad. Buddy looked at his watch – three forty-five. Where had he been all this time? He had never been this late before.

After a minute, his dad walked past the door. Buddy wanted to call out but perhaps his dad would be angry if he asked any questions. At least he was home now. Was Mr Rybeero home yet or was he still driving through the dark streets? Maybe Charmian and Julius had just been woken up by him as he came in from work. The only difference was they would know where their dad had been until so late, and he didn't.

## Chapter Eight

Buddy got up at eight thirty, had breakfast and started cleaning the rooms downstairs. It took him ages and they still didn't look as good as when his mum did them. It was an improvement, though – especially the kitchen, which had been in a terrible state. When his dad finally staggered downstairs at twelve fifteen, Buddy asked, 'What do you think?'

'I think I want a cuppa tea,' his dad said, rubbing his eyes.

'No, the cleaning, I've done all the rooms.'

'You must be thirsty, then. So make some tea.'

Buddy made the tea and sat down at the table, feeling a bit disappointed. His dad sipped the tea then looked around the room.

'Make a good charlady, you would. 'Ow much d'you charge?'

Buddy smiled – his dad was pleased after all.

'No, come on –'ow much?'

'Nothing,' Buddy laughed.

'Blimey, don't never do nothing for nothing, mate. Let's see . . . I reckon it's worth . . . a tenner?' He reached into his trouser pocket and took out a bundle of notes. He peeled off two £5 notes and put them down in front of Buddy. 'Go on – they're yours. Plenty more where that came from. And we'll go down the shops later. Get you some trousers.'

Buddy could hardly believe it but one look at his dad's smiling face told him it was true. 'Where did you . . .' he began, but his dad tapped him on the cheek – it was a friendly pat but hard.

'Ask no questions and I won't tell you no lies. I'm working, right? Now shut your gob and pour us another cup.'

His dad was in great spirits. He put a Buddy Holly LP on and turned it up really loud. The music boomed round the house while they both went upstairs to get ready.

'Make sure you've got clean underpants,' his dad shouted. 'Don't want you showing me up in the shops. My old mum used to say, "Terry, always make sure your undies are clean. If you get knocked down by a car, I don't want the doctors thinking I let you run around dirty." Poor old dear meant it, too. Bless her heart.'

They stopped off at a pub on the way to the shops. Buddy was going to wait outside but his dad told him to come in with him. The pub was crowded but there was a table near the door. Buddy sat there while his dad went to the bar to get the drinks.

'There you go,' his dad said, putting down a half-pint for Buddy and a pint for himself.

'It's beer,' Buddy whispered.

'Course it is – it's a pub, ain't it?'

Buddy would have preferred a Coke but he sipped his beer and pretended to enjoy it. His dad even offered him a cigarette but he didn't take it.

'That's right, son, you stay off 'em. At your age I was on twenty a day; now I can't stop,' his dad said with a laugh as he lit up. 'Lovely, though, eh?'

Buddy liked the noisy, smoky atmosphere and the way his dad was treating him like a grown-up. He took a big gulp of his beer and finished it.

'Right little boozer, ain't you?' his dad said and went back to the bar for some more. He came back with two pints for himself, another half-pint for Buddy and four packets of crisps.

'Didn't know what flavour so I bought 'em all.'

When they left the pub, the bright sunshine made Buddy squint and he walked along the street feeling slightly light-headed. Everything his dad said made him laugh. In the first clothes shop they came to, his dad took a pair of bright yellow trousers from the rack and held them up. Buddy got such a fit of giggles that they had to leave.

In the next shop, Buddy picked out a pair of very ordinary grey trousers and tried them on.

'Bit boring, ain't they?' his dad said when Buddy came out of the changing cubicle. 'Why don't you buy some nice drainpipes like these?' he asked, pointing to his own trousers that were so narrow that they kept riding up over his pink socks.

'They're for school, Dad.'

'Blimey, my son's a right square,' his dad said to the shop assistant. 'Now, what else you want?' His dad made him buy a couple of shirts and a sweater. Buddy thought of mentioning the parka – it really was too small – but his dad had spent enough already. After all, how long would this job last? It certainly paid well whatever it was. All sorts of questions about the job still buzzed in his head but he tried to push them away.

They walked along the streets looking at the shops and his dad talked happily about how he would soon be able to get his bike back.

'You never know – might even get another record shop. That'd be a bit of all right, wouldn't it?'

That would be great. Buddy could still remember the tiny shop filled with records. There'd been posters of Elvis and Buddy and other rock 'n' roll singers and the shop had been loud with music. Rock 'n' roll fans, lots of them dressed – like his dad – in Teddy boy clothes, had come from miles away to talk, listen to the music and buy rare records of the fifties. It had been more like a club than a shop and his dad had been really happy.

Then, one night, it had burned down. Everything had been destroyed. Buddy had only been eight at the time but he could still remember the look on his dad's face when he'd heard the news. They'd all rushed round there and stood looking at the gaping, charred hole where the shop had been. During the fire the records had melted. As the vinyl had cooled, it had set into a hard, black stream that flowed across the pavement and into the gutter. There, in the middle of the road, a terrible row had started when his mum found out that his dad had never bothered to insure the shop. It must have been the first bad row between them that Buddy had ever heard, because even now it made him shudder.

Oh yes, it would be terrific if his dad could start another shop like that.

Oddly enough, though, this sudden hope for the future made Buddy nervous. It hadn't been long after the shop had burned down that his dad had gone to prison. If only he could be sure that he wasn't doing something that might get him into trouble. The thought nagged him all the rest of the afternoon and while they were having tea Buddy finally plucked up the courage to say something.

'Mrs Rybeero told me they need taxi drivers.'

'You're too young to drive, big-boots.'

'Not me. Don't muck around. I meant you.'

'Me? Working for blacks? You're 'aving a laugh.'

'Why?'

'Because they're black, stupid!'

'You're just racist!'

'Yeah? So what?'

'Anyway, that's not the point. It's a good job.'

'But what?' His dad put down his knife and fork and glared at him.

Buddy longed to go on – to ask what the job was, to beg him not to do anything that might send him back to prison – but he didn't.

'I don't get you,' his dad said. 'First you moan 'cos we ain't got no money, then you moan when I make a bit. You got your trousers, didn't you?'

'I'm not moaning,' Buddy mumbled.

They finished their meal in silence and Buddy felt awful. His dad was doing it all for him and he wasn't even grateful. All he did was criticize. Not just about this. It was everything. Things his dad did irritated him – like the noise he made eating and drinking, the unusual clothes he wore, the swaggering way he walked. Why couldn't he be more like other kids' dads?

Yet he didn't always think like that. There were times when he loved the fact that his dad was different. He liked it when he mucked around and he was glad that he wasn't like Mr Normington and people of that sort. It was all so confusing. Sometimes these opposite feelings swirled about inside Buddy's mind until he wished he could open his head like a window and let it all go flying out.

# Chapter Nine

His dad went out again that night and the next night, too. Buddy tried not to worry but it was hard and he was glad when Monday came and there was school to think about. The twins – Julius in particular – were still going on about the house at Croxley Street but Buddy didn't take much notice. It all seemed silly compared with other things.

Mr Normington was away again on the Monday, but on the Tuesday he was back. At the end of morning registration he stopped Buddy on the way out of the classroom.

'Now, lad, that's a bit more like it, isn't it?' he said, nodding at Buddy's trousers.

Buddy was ashamed at how much pleasure he got from this word of approval. He didn't like Mr Normington but he had deliberately waited until most people had left the room and then walked past the teacher's desk hoping that he'd be noticed.

'That bag still makes you look a bit of a scruff, though,' Mr Normington added, pointing to the plastic bag.

Buddy's face burned with embarrassment, especially when David Siddell and Emma Groves went by humming 'My Old Man's a Dustman'.

'Still, any improvement is better than none,' Mr Normington said casually and tapped him on the side of the head with a book as a sign for him to go.

Out in the corridor, Buddy caught up with David Siddell and Emma Groves. He got hold of Siddell's shoulder and swung him round.

'Just watch it, Siddell.'

As soon as he spoke, Buddy realized he'd made a mistake. What could he say? Don't sing that song? It would sound ridiculous.

'Watch what?' Siddell said and brushed his shoulder as if Buddy's hands had been filthy.

'They're so violent, aren't they?' Emma Groves said, as if Buddy were some kind of primitive animal. Buddy hated her piercing, snobby voice. He felt like punching her stupid, round face and sending her back to her precious family with a black eye and a squashed nose.

'Just watch it, that's all,' he said feebly and started down the corridor. Siddell stuck out his foot and Buddy tripped over it. He stumbled but stopped himself from falling, then swung round, whirling his plastic bag in the direction of Siddell's head. Siddell was too quick, though. He grabbed the plastic bag with his free hand and jabbed his black briefcase hard into Buddy's stomach with the other.

Buddy fell back against the wall, gasping for breath. The plastic bag ripped and all his books fell to the floor. He was left leaning against the wall, with just the tattered ends of the white plastic in his hands. Emma Groves' laughter floated back along the corridor.

He brooded over it all morning. It served him right for wanting Mr Normington to notice the trousers. But the really sickening thing was that he wanted a proper school bag more than ever. He told himself he didn't care what Siddell and Groves and Mr Normington thought – but it wasn't true.

As soon as he got home from school, he took out the £10 his dad had given him and went to the shops. He bought a big, red, canvas shoulder bag. He'd still be different from Siddell and that crowd with their hard, black briefcases – he didn't want to be like them – but at least Mr Normington couldn't call him a scruff now.

His dad stayed at home on Tuesday and Wednesday evenings and Buddy felt much happier. Apart from the fact that the house wasn't lonely and scary when his dad was there, he half hoped that the 'work' had stopped. It would mean an end to the money, of course, but it would be worth it if it ended the worry. On Thursday, though, his dad went out and the worrying began again.

Then, on Friday morning, there was a discussion in the General Studies lesson about crime. Buddy tried to close his ears but he couldn't stop hearing things people said. They were going on about how criminals should be made to pay with long prison sentences and that prison should be like the old days with chains and whips. Some people even suggested that thieves ought to have their hands cut off like in some Arab countries. The crazy thing was that a lot of these opinions came from people who, Buddy knew, had nicked things from shops. It was as if they didn't realize that they were thieves, too. And it was also obvious that they'd never had to worry about their dads going to prison.

Buddy felt uneasy and depressed for the rest of the day. He didn't even enjoy the Satellite Club that evening. In fact, he left early and hurried home to check whether his dad was in. Luckily, he was – lying on the sofa listening to records. As Buddy came through the door, though, his dad jumped as if startled and slid something behind a cushion.

Buddy pretended not to notice but as soon as his dad left the room, he went over and felt behind the cushion. He found a photograph of his mum.

When he got to bed, he couldn't sleep. The photo must mean that his dad still missed her. They never mentioned her now but Buddy had never stopped thinking about her. Sometimes he daydreamed about her coming back. Once, he'd nearly asked his dad for her new address so he could go and talk to her. In the end, he hadn't – partly because he thought his dad would be angry or upset, but mainly because he'd feel too ashamed to face her.

He knew now, of course, that it couldn't have been all his fault. There must have been other things wrong – that's why his mum and dad had argued so much. But the money he'd stolen from her purse had been the thing that had finally made her leave. Perhaps, if he hadn't done that, she would still be here and his dad wouldn't have to look secretly at her photo.

What was she doing? Did she still work as a secretary in that office? Perhaps he could wait outside the building one evening to see her come out. Did she think about them sometimes? Did she hate him?

The thoughts kept him awake for ages and he slept until nearly eleven o'clock the next morning. His dad was already up and getting ready to go out.

'Meeting someone,' he said. 'Won't be back till late. Need any money?'

Buddy shook his head but his dad put £5 on the table anyway.

After his dad left, the house seemed empty and depressing. He turned the radio up loud while he had some breakfast and then went upstairs to get dressed. Although it was daytime, he was suddenly scared. He kept feeling as if there were somebody behind him, and he even bent down and checked there was nobody under the bed.

He wasn't due at the twins' house until two but he decided to leave early. Better to take his time walking rather than stay here alone. He switched off the radio and stood for a moment in the silence then dashed along the corridor and out of the front door.

As soon as he was outside, he felt better. He walked slowly along the roads in the sunshine and could laugh at himself for having been so scared.

Mrs Rybeero was, as usual, at the desk when Buddy walked into the office. She was talking on the phone but she waved at him and pointed to the back room.

'Buddy, you'll never guess what!' Julius shouted as soon as he saw him.

'Ssh!' Charmian said quickly and leapt up to make sure the door to the office was properly closed.

'What is it?' Buddy whispered and his heart began to race.

'We had a phone call this morning,' Julius began.

'Keep your voice down, Jules,' Charmian hissed and pulled them both into the kitchen before she went on. 'Mum was out shopping so we had to look after the office. I was on the phone taking the messages and Julius was on the radio to the taxis.'

'And she forgot to take the address and . . .' Julius broke in.

Charmian put her hand over Julius's mouth. 'I'm telling it! Someone rang up for a taxi and I forgot to ask them for their address.'

'And then she said I'd have to answer if they rang up again,' Julius said, breaking free of Charmian, 'but I told her to get lost.'

'Jules, please – let me tell it.'

'OK, OK – just get on with it,' Julius said, sitting on the table out of reach of his sister.

'Anyway,' Charmian went on, 'Jules said he wouldn't answer if they rang back, so when the phone went a couple of minutes later, I had to pick it up. I was all ready to apologize, but it wasn't the same person. It was someone else, asking for a taxi to go to the docks. Well, after the last one, I wasn't going to make the same mistake so I asked for the address.' Charmian paused dramatically. 'It was 56 Croxley Street.'

Buddy felt the hair rise on the back of his neck and he looked at Julius, who nodded and said, 'It's true. I heard it.'

'I thought I was hearing things so I asked the man to repeat it and Jules listened in.'

'What did you do?' Buddy asked.

'Right, now it's my bit,' Julius began, jumping off the table and almost acting out the story. 'So, I called the taxis, see. Everyone was busy except Delgado, so he went. Then, about half an hour later, Delgado dropped in here to say he was going to have a couple of hours' break so I thought I'd ask him some questions, all casual like.'

'You should've seen him,' Charmian laughed. 'He thinks he's a real smoothie detective.'

'Get lost! I had to be careful or he'd have got suspicious. Anyway, I found out loads. Del picked up the bloke outside number 56 – he was waiting on the pavement. A short bloke, very fat. Black coat, white hair and big thick glasses. And he was carrying a suitcase. Del helped him with it and it weighed a ton. He went to the docks and got out at a pub. Don't you think it's great? I told you there was something weird going on but you two wouldn't listen.'

Buddy had to admit that the whole thing was a strange coincidence. And there were all sorts of mysteries, such as what was in the case, and why was there a phone in a house that was all boarded up? On the other hand, he couldn't really share the excitement that even Charmian seemed to feel. After all, what could they do?

There was no stopping Julius, though. He wanted to go back to Croxley Street and see if they could find out more. Charmian agreed, saying that there wasn't much else to do and it might be good fun. They both nagged him until he said he'd go with them but he wasn't happy about it. There was something about that house that scared him – something that reminded him about all his fears of death. In some strange way, the house was dangerous.

# Chapter Ten

Even in the daytime number 56 Croxley Street looked sinister. It was built of dark stone that had been stained darker in places where rain had dripped down from the broken gutters. From the grey slates of the roof down to the ground there was no lightness or colour anywhere. The trees and bushes in the garden were a miserable dark green that seemed to swallow up the light. Buddy noticed that where the branches of one of the bushes leaned against the stone of the house, the leaves had died as though poisoned by its touch.

The worst thing of all were the boards on the windows. They were what made the whole place look so gloomy and lifeless, and anyone could be inside peering out through the cracks. Buddy stepped back behind the large, brick gatepost. 'Now what?' he said. 'There's nothing to see.'

'How about going round the back?'

'No, Jules,' Charmian said at once, grabbing hold of her brother's arm.

'Why not?'

'We might get caught, that's why. Tell him, Buddy.'

'Well, I'm not going,' Buddy said. 'The whole place gives me the creeps. I told you it wasn't worth coming.'

'You two are just scared,' Julius said, then jerked his arm free. He darted away through the gate and into the garden.

'Julius!' Charmian called out, but there was no answer. 'Honestly, that kid. Come on – we can't let him go alone.' She peered round the gatepost, then ran into the garden.

Buddy hesitated. If it were any other house, he wouldn't have minded. It could be good fun sneaking into back gardens – he'd done it loads of times when he was a kid. But this house . . . Anyway, he didn't feel like a kid any more. Julius had been right, he was scared. Nowadays, he was worried and scared half the time so there was no pleasure in scaring himself on purpose.

Suddenly, Julius came dashing out of the gate. He pushed Buddy back against the gatepost and burst out laughing.

'Some old bird's caught Charmian!'

'What?'

'I was hiding just inside the hedge here and she went belting past looking for me. Then this old lady opened the window.'

'In the house?'

'No – next door.'

Buddy peeped round the gatepost. Charmian was standing at the entrance to the dark alleyway that led down towards the back garden of number 56. She was looking up at the side wall of the house next door. There was an open window and Buddy could see that the lace curtains had been pulled aside but he couldn't see who was there. Charmian said something, pointed out to the road, then nodded. She glanced quickly down the side of 56 then turned and ran towards the gate.

'Where were you?' she said angrily to Julius.

'Behind the hedge. Did she tell you off?'

Charmian shook her head. 'She wants to tell me something.'

'You're not going, are you?' Buddy asked.

'She said it was important.'

As Charmian started along the pavement, Julius raised his arms wide and looked at Buddy in disbelief. When Charmian reached the gate of 54 she turned and beckoned to them.

'She's nuts,' Julius said.

Buddy waited a moment, hoping that she'd change her mind, but when she signalled again and went through the gate, he and Julius followed. As they scrambled up the tall flight of steps to the front door, Charmian was already ringing the bell.

'What does she want?' Buddy asked, hoping that it would turn out to be something harmless like an errand that she needed done.

'I don't know. She asked me if I liked cats and then said she had something important to say.'

'Yeah – probably wants us to clear up some cat's mess on her carpet,' Julius said.

Charmian rang the bell again. In the silence after the bell, they could hear squeaking noises coming towards them along the corridor.

'Sounds as if she needs oiling,' Julius whispered and they all started to giggle.

'Ssh!' Charmian said, trying to control herself, but that made them giggle even more. There was the sound of three bolts being drawn slowly back and then the rattle of a chain. This was too much for Julius, who started to snort and choke.

The door swung open slowly to reveal an old lady sitting in a wheelchair. Buddy was aware of three pairs of eyes – the pale blue ones of the old lady and the large green ones of the two black cats on her lap. The old lady's eyes flicked nervously from Buddy to the twins, then past them in the direction of Number 56.

A terrible stench of fish wafted out of the door and Buddy glanced along the corridor to the filthy-looking kitchen at the end. The floor was covered with rubbish and there was a large saucepan bubbling away on the stove.

'You're the ones who were round here the other night, aren't you?' the old lady suddenly whispered hoarsely.

Buddy started to deny it but Charmian nodded.

'Yes, well, you're very silly children,' the old lady went on, her voice rising angrily. 'You could get yourselves hurt, you know. I was going to warn you then, but I never open my door at night. Old people like me get mugged every day. Worse than that sometimes.'

There was a splutter from Julius and he ducked behind Charmian to hide.

The old lady turned on him angrily. 'Don't you snigger, young man. You'd laugh on the other side of your face if he caught you in his garden.'

'Who?' Charmian asked.

'The Beast – that's who. It's nearly four – time for his walk. He ought to be under lock and key, not walking the streets. This used to be a nice neighbourhood before they let him loose to frighten us all. They ought to put him back before he kills someone.'

The old lady's voice was so fierce that even Julius stopped laughing. He glanced across towards the next house and then back to the old lady as if he wasn't quite sure whether she was serious or not. Buddy wasn't sure either. It sounded weird but there wasn't a trace of a joke in her voice.

'What does he do?' Julius said.

'Go and find out, if you think it's so funny,' she snapped. 'He strangles cats and he'd probably do the same to you – and good riddance.'

There was an awkward silence after this outburst. Then Charmian spoke, 'My brother didn't mean to laugh – he just gets giggly.'

The old lady shrugged sulkily but the apology seemed to have calmed her down.

'Does he really strangle cats?' Charmian asked.

'He killed my Katerina, didn't he? Out there.' She pointed down the alleyway. 'Then he held up her poor little body to taunt me. I saw him from my window. I see everything from there. I know what goes on. He'd kill Ida and Grace, too, if I gave him half a chance. But mummy won't let him, will she, my lovelies?' she said, lifting the two cats and kissing their heads.

Buddy could see Julius biting his lip, desperately trying not to smile. Charmian's face, though, was full of concern. 'Why didn't you tell the police?' she asked.

'Pooh, the police – what do they care? I rang them when those lazy dustmen kept dropping rubbish down my path. What did they do? Nothing. "Too busy," they said.'

'But this is different. Killing a cat – that's awful.'

The old lady's face softened and she smiled up at Charmian, showing her yellowy false teeth. 'There, I knew you'd understand. We know straightaway when somebody loves us, don't we, my lovelies? Yes, we do. Say hello to the nice young lady, girls.' She held up the two cats and waggled their paws. 'This is Grace. And this is Ida. And I'm Mrs Solomon.'

Charmian shook hands and told Mrs Solomon her name. The old lady smiled and gushed on about how pleased she was but when Buddy and Julius introduced themselves she nodded briefly without a smile and turned back to talk to Charmian. Julius raised his eyebrows at Buddy to show what he thought, then leaned against the porch wall. Buddy went down a couple of steps and peered along the passageway towards the back garden of number 56. There was an area of cracked and uneven concrete near the end of the alley and, beyond that, long, unkempt grass and overgrown bushes that were as neglected as the house.

Charmian was now crouching down, stroking the cats while Mrs Solomon told her what they liked to eat and what funny tricks they got up to. Julius yawned loudly and tapped his feet against the wall. Buddy was just about to sit down on the edge of the steps when a tall figure turned the corner from the back of number 56.

He jumped up on the porch and whispered urgently, 'It's him – that beast person.'

'I told you – every day at four o'clock,' Mrs Solomon said triumphantly.

There was the sound of dragging footsteps, then the man came into view. The porch was so high that even though he was very tall, they were looking down on his head. It was impossible to see what he looked like because he was wearing an old-fashioned leather cap with a large peak and earflaps that covered the sides of his face. He walked slowly, his shoulders hunched and his hands thrust deep into the pockets of his long, black overcoat.

As the man shuffled towards the front gate, Buddy was startled by a shout from Mrs Solomon. 'Murderer!'

The man stopped and slowly turned towards them. The white face and the dark-ringed eyes were unmistakable – it was the man they'd seen through the letterbox. He opened his mouth to say something but Mrs Solomon didn't give him a chance.

'I saw you!' she shouted. 'I know all about you – don't think I don't. Comings and goings in the middle of the night. Killing innocent animals. Beast!'

The man's mouth moved but no sound came out. He stayed like that for a moment then made his way out of the gate and along the road.

'Does he live on his own?' Julius asked when the man finally went out of sight behind a distant hedge.

'Who'd live with him?' Mrs Solomon asked crossly. Then she took Charmian's hand and said in a much gentler voice, 'I told you he'd come, didn't I? So don't you go hanging round there any more – especially not at night. It's not safe for a young girl like you.'

Julius looked at Buddy and flicked his eyes quickly in the direction of the road. 'Well, we'd better go now,' he said casually.

Mrs Solomon must have heard but she didn't even glance at them so Buddy followed Julius down the steps, along the path and out on to the pavement. When they looked back, Charmian was still talking to Mrs Solomon. Far off, down near the end of the road, Buddy could just make out the figure of the Beast.

'What about going round the back – now he's out?' Julius asked. 'Come on, it'll be a laugh.'

The same idea had occurred to Buddy – except it wasn't for a laugh. What Mrs Solomon had said about 'comings and goings in the night' had started his brain racing. Something that had been nagging away at the back of his mind had suddenly become clear. Somehow or other, the mystery of his dad's work could be tied up with this house.

Now he'd made the connection, Buddy couldn't understand why he hadn't seen it before – it was so obvious. His dad had mentioned the house the same night he'd first talked about the job. It wasn't the sort of story you came out with like that – not unless someone had just told it to you. So, who would have told his dad the story? The same person who'd offered him the work, of course.

It could just be a coincidence – and he hoped it was; but either way, he had to find out. Now was the perfect opportunity and the last thing he wanted was for Julius to go charging in there on his own.

'OK – but we'd better wait till Charmian comes.'

'Great stuff!' Julius said, and then called, 'Get a move on, Char!'

Charmian waved her hand in acknowledgement then bent down and gave the cats a final stroke. Mrs Solomon said something to her before wheeling her chair backwards and closing the door. Buddy could imagine all the locks being turned and the chains being replaced.

'What's the big hurry?' Charmian said when she came through the gate.

'We're going in there while the Beast's out,' Buddy said, and he and Julius ran along the pavement and into the garden of 56 before she had the chance to argue.

# Chapter Eleven

The back of the house was as dreary as the front even though the stonework had been painted white at one time. Damp had risen from the ground and stained the peeling paint with a green mould.

The three steps that led down to the back door were shiny with damp. To the right of the door was a window that, like those at the front, had been boarded up. Just to the left of the door, though, about seven feet from the ground was a small window that not only had no boards on it but was actually half open. Buddy took a couple of steps backwards then ran and jumped. He caught hold of the windowsill.

'Give me a bunk-up.'

'Buddy – don't,' Charmian called.

'Look, stop moaning,' grunted Julius as he took hold of Buddy's legs and pushed him upwards. 'If you're going to stay here, belt up, or go back and talk to that old crone.'

Buddy swung the window outwards and hauled himself up until his head and shoulders were through the hole. He was now blocking most of the light but he could see that the small room had been some kind of larder. There were shelves on the left and a door on the right which must lead into the corridor next to the back door.

'OK, Jules, let go. I'll go in and open the back door.'

He kicked his legs and started to squirm through. It was a tight squeeze and he grazed his shin, but finally he managed to pull his body through. Balancing with one hand on the shelf and the other on the window ledge, he jumped to the floor. His leg stung like mad. He lifted his jeans and wiped a trickle of blood from the graze.

He was just reaching for the doorknob when it started to turn. Someone was in the house. He sprang round and leaped for the window. His hands slipped and he tumbled backwards on to the floor.

Julius was grinning down at him. 'The back door wasn't locked.'

Buddy took a few seconds to get his breath back then let Julius pull him to his feet. He followed him out into the corridor where Charmian was slowly opening another door opposite. The room was in semi-darkness because of the boards on the window. Buddy tried the switch just inside the door but no light came on. In the corner near the window he could just make out an old-fashioned, shallow stone sink into which a tap dripped softly. Along the far wall an ancient gas stove lay on its side as if someone had disconnected it and then let it drop.

'This must be where he sleeps,' Charmian said in a rather scared voice.

Buddy turned and looked at the camp bed that stood against the wall behind the door. There were a couple of blankets on it and a rolled-up sweater that obviously served as a pillow. All along the bed stood candles of various sizes. Was the Beast scared of the dark? At the far end of the bed was a pile of cans. Charmian went over and peered down at them.

'Stewed steak. Peas. Potato salad. He must eat them cold,' she said, picking up a half-empty can with a fork in it. She shivered and put it down.

'Do you think he stays here all the time?' Julius whispered.

'Don't know. Let's have a look at the rest of the house.' Buddy turned and hit his knee on the edge of the door. His leg was going to be in a bad state by the end of the day.

There was another empty cupboard next to the larder, then three steps that led up to the main part of the house. Buddy walked up them and gently opened the door at the top. There was a large, tiled entrance hall with a wide staircase leading upstairs. Buddy glanced up the stairs then crossed the hall to the front door. This was where the Beast had been that night they'd looked through the letterbox.

The front room on the right of the hall was a mess. The wallpaper was hanging off the walls and there were chunks of fallen plaster on the floor. The room on the left of the hall, though, looked as if someone had swept it recently. It was completely empty except that in the middle of the bare floorboards there was a telephone.

'Why put it there?' Charmian asked.

'Why have one at all?' Julius answered. 'The whole place is weird. I wonder where he killed her?'

Buddy had been so concerned about looking for any sign that might connect his dad with the house that he'd completely forgotten about the murder. He suddenly found himself peering at the floorboards as if he might find bloodstains on them.

Julius led the way up the staircase to the first floor. Buddy and Charmian stopped halfway up and looked over the banister to the hall below. There was a chink of glass and Buddy glanced up and saw Julius stumble. A bottle shot out from under his foot and came tumbling down towards them. Buddy tried to stop it but it caught the edge of the stair above him and flipped over his hand. It sailed in a high arc and shattered on the tiles of the hall. The crash could have been heard out in the street.

In the silence afterwards, they all held their breath.

'Blimey, this is scary,' Julius said at last. 'Let's have a quick look up here then get out.'

All five rooms were empty. The dust choked Buddy's nose and the dark corners of the rooms gave him the shivers. Once, when he stood still, he could hear soft rustlings under the floorboards.

Buddy was all prepared to go when Charmian opened a small door next to the bathroom and found a narrow staircase. The stairs curved up to an attic with steep, sloping ceilings. Julius pointed to a large hook screwed into the beam that ran from one end of the room to the other. He didn't need to say anything; they were all thinking the same thing – perhaps this was where the man had hanged himself.

Despite these thoughts about the house's past, though, Buddy felt pleased. This was the last room and he hadn't seen a sign that there was anything suspicious going on. True, it was a bit strange for someone to live in one dirty room and leave the rest of the house empty – and that telephone was odd – but lots of people led really weird lives. Meths drinkers, for instance – they lived in worse places than this. He'd heard of people who never threw anything away and whose houses were piled high with junk and rubbish so that you couldn't even sit down. No, there was nothing to connect his dad with this house except that he'd told an interesting story about it.

There were high windows at either end of the attic and Buddy went to the one that overlooked the front. There was a wooden box seat set into the wall below the window and he stepped up on to it. As he wiped the dust from the window a huge spider scuttled over the glass. He sprang back and nearly fell from the seat. The spider squeezed itself into a long crack in the wall and Buddy leaned forward again.

The sky had filled with a solid screen of black cloud and big drops of rain were beginning to splatter the pavement. A sudden scurry of wind brought the rain beating down so heavily that the houses across the street became just dim shapes. Something moved in the garden and Buddy craned his neck to get a better view. The Beast was walking fast across the lawn.

'It's him,' he yelled and all three of them dived for the stairs. Buddy was almost at the bottom when Julius slipped and crashed into him, knocking him forward into Charmian. They tumbled down the last couple of steps and landed in a heap. In an instant they were up and running along the hallway.

They were halfway down the main stairs when the back door slammed. They froze and listened. There was a shuffling sound, then silence. Buddy's blood boomed in his ears. Had the Beast gone into the kitchen? If he noticed that the door to the main part of the house was open, he might come up and see the broken bottle.

Buddy leaned over the banister. He could just see the doorway that led down to the kitchen. It was empty. There was a clatter of tins – he must be in the kitchen. If they could get down to the hall without making any noise, there was a chance that they could rush past the kitchen and out of the back door before the Beast knew what was happening.

He began tiptoeing down the stairs and the twins followed. At every step the boards creaked terribly, no matter how carefully they trod. Buddy's hands were sticky with sweat and he felt a trickle roll from his armpit down his side. At last they reached the bottom and began to pick their way carefully through the shattered glass.

There was a loud clatter of cans. Julius made a funny, squeaking cry of fright and ran to the front door. He turned the handle and pulled but it didn't open. Buddy stood helplessly as Julius panicked and began to rattle the door in desperation.

Charmian grabbed Buddy's arm, her eyes wide with fear. The Beast was coming out of the kitchen. He was carrying a knife.

Buddy's first instinct was to bolt upstairs or into one of the rooms off the hall but Charmian pulled him in the direction of the front door. Julius stopped rattling the door and they huddled together, staring at the Beast who was now on the top step of the little flight of stairs. He was so tall that his head nearly touched the door frame.

The greyish-white skin was drawn so tightly over his bones that his face looked like a skull. His black hair was roughly cut and a long strand of it flapped over his sunken, red-rimmed eyes. Deep lines curved down from the sides of his nose and joined the sad creases at the edge of his mouth. His pale, moist lips opened.

'What you doing?' The Beast's voice was deep but he spoke quietly and there was a slight pause between each word.

All sorts of mad explanations flew through Buddy's head but before he could say a word he was astonished to hear Charmian's voice, loud and steady, demand, 'Why did you strangle the cat?'

The effect was extraordinary. Despite his size, the Beast suddenly looked like a little boy. His eyes grew wide and his lower lip began to tremble.

'Didn't. Didn't kill him.' His voice almost broke with emotion. 'Found him. Put him in a hole. Lady didn't want him.'

Buddy had never been so sure that someone was telling the truth. The reply was so direct and innocent that it couldn't be a lie.

The Beast suddenly looked down at the knife then lowered his arm and tried to hide it behind his back.

'Never killed him,' he said and shook his head.

'That's all right, then,' Charmian said more gently. 'We'll go and tell the lady you didn't.' There was a pause then she added, 'Would you like that?'

The Beast nodded slowly, then mumbled something.

'Pardon?' Charmian said.

'Mr King says no one can come in here,' he said more clearly.

'Well, we won't come in again. We just wanted to find out about the cat, that's all. OK?' Charmian's voice was still very cool and controlled but Buddy felt her tremble.

'OK?' she said again.

The Beast nodded. Charmian started forward and Julius and Buddy followed her. For a moment Buddy was worried that the Beast would change his mind but when they got to him, he stepped aside and let them pass. They walked quickly down the steps and along the corridor to the back door. Julius opened it and he and Charmian dashed out to freedom. Buddy controlled his urge to run and he turned when he got to the door. The Beast was still standing in the hall, his head lowered as if in disgrace.

'We'll tell her you didn't do it,' Buddy called.

The Beast didn't move. The Beast. What a ridiculous name for someone as helpless-looking as this man.

'What's your name?' Buddy asked.

'Ralph James Campbell.' It was said like a child who has learned it in case he ever got lost and Buddy wouldn't have been surprised if he'd added his address.

'Goodbye, Mr Campbell.'

Buddy closed the door quietly and, despite the rain, he didn't bother to run.

# Chapter Twelve

Buddy was glad that the twins asked him back to their place because, in addition to the fact that there was so much to talk about, he didn't really fancy spending the evening alone at home.

They spent ages going over all the events and it was amazing how differently they remembered things. Julius swore that the Beast had been holding a can opener, not a knife, and that the telephone had been in the room next to the stairs. Charmian hadn't even noticed anything in the Beast's hand and she was sure that the telephone had been in the room opposite the stairs.

There was a big argument over the name of the man that the Beast had mentioned. Buddy and Charmian said it was 'Mr King' but Julius was certain that it was 'Mr Keg'.

'It was "Keg", I know it was,' Julius said stubbornly. 'Anyway, I bet it was the fat bloke that called for the taxi.'

Buddy wanted to know what on earth had given Charmian the bright idea of accusing the Beast of strangling the cat but she said she'd just blurted out the first thing she could think of. All three of them, though, agreed about one thing – the Beast had been telling the truth when he'd said he hadn't done it.

Buddy and Julius both thought that Mrs Solomon was a nosy troublemaker who'd exaggerated the story simply because she didn't like the Beast. Charmian, on the other hand, said she was just a frightened old lady and that if the Beast had shaken the dead body when he'd held it up it could easily have looked as if he was strangling it.

'Look,' she said when Julius called Mrs Solomon yet another rude name. 'Who went back afterwards? Me, not you – and she practically admitted she could've made a mistake. The only thing she was bothered about was if I'd go round and talk to her sometimes. She's lonely, that's all.'

'Yeah, well, you're welcome to go round and see that crazy old nutter,' Julius said.

Buddy stayed with the twins as late as he could, hoping that his dad might be back by the time he got home, but he wasn't. The house was dark and empty and he had a hard job not giving in to the kind of panic he'd had that morning.

He tried to think positively – the Beast, for instance, had seemed to be scary but he'd turned out to be a bit pathetic.

And that sudden worry about number 56 and his dad's work – that had been a false alarm, hadn't it? It would probably turn out that his dad wasn't doing anything wrong, after all.

Thinking like that helped a bit and he even managed to find the courage to switch off his bedroom light when he went to bed.

He was in that house. It was very dark. He was alone. He was floating in and out of the rooms. Outside, in the garden, people were shouting and throwing stones at the windows. There were no boards at the windows and he could hear the glass shattering.

The noise stopped and he was floating through the house again.

He was going upstairs. Slowly. If he went into any of the rooms, he knew what he would find. There were old newspapers on the bare floorboards of the upstairs corridor. They were there to stop the blood from going on the floor.

The door that led to the attic was open and he could see the end of a thick piece of rope. It moved upwards slowly, step by step. It was being pulled by someone – the man who killed his wife. Perhaps he could ring his mum and ask her to come – but the phone was in that room. He couldn't go in there. The body might be in there. Which body? The cat's body? No, worse than that. The Beast was on the stairs. Buddy floated down to him. The Beast opened his mouth and something black flicked across his lips. Was his tongue black? It wasn't a tongue, it was the tip of a tail. A centipede's tail.

The Beast reached up and grabbed hold of it and it wriggled between his fingers. He started to pull and, inch by inch, the body started to come out, hundreds of legs writhing at the sides. It was huge – as wide as a tie. The Beast was dragging it out of his mouth like a sailor pulling on a rope. Hand after hand. Yards of it. Black, scaly, shining with the juices from the Beast's throat. And, at last, the head was there – its jaws pinched tight on something pink. It was the Beast's stomach. The centipede was fixed to it and if the Beast kept pulling, he would turn himself inside out. Buddy screamed and the Beast let go. The centipede shot back down inside him.

Buddy screamed again and again. Then he woke up, still screaming. His body was burning and the sleeping bag was soaking with sweat.

The bedroom light flashed on and his dad was there.

'Hey, what's up? What's up? Ssh! Ssh! It's only a dream.'

Buddy started to cry and his dad sat down on the bed. Buddy hugged him. His dad tried to push him away but Buddy hung on tight round his neck.

'I thought you were out.'

'I been back ages. Didn't 'alf give me a turn – I was fast asleep.'

'I had a nightmare.'

'You ain't kidding – must've woken up 'alf the street. 'Ere, let go of us – you're all wet.'

Buddy let go and his dad stood up.

'You'd better take that T-shirt off. You got any clean?'

His dad opened a drawer and rummaged around, turning everything upside down.

'I think they're all dirty,' Buddy said.

'Better wear this football shirt, then. Can dream you're playing at Wembley instead of 'aving nightmares. What was it about – monsters?'

Buddy shrugged and put the shirt on. He wished he could talk about the dream to his dad but he couldn't.

'Right, you'd better kip down again. We'll go down the launderette tomorrow – together, eh? Get a bit of washing done.'

Buddy nodded and lay down.

'You all right, then?' his dad said and he leaned over and ruffled Buddy's hair. 'You look like a brush. Skinhead!'

'Teddy boy!'

'Proud of it, too.' His dad smiled and turned off the light.

'Leave the door open, Dad.'

'Blimey, what a baby,' his dad said but he didn't close the door and he left the light on in the corridor, too.

His dad teased him terribly all the next day. He kept singing the old Buddy Holly song 'Moondreams' in a funny 'ghost' voice, and trying to scare him by tapping him on the shoulder when he wasn't looking. Buddy didn't mind, though, because his dad was in such a good mood. He messed around like mad in the launderette, pretending he didn't know how to work the machine and getting an old lady to help him.

While their clothes were washing, they went round the corner to the nearest pub and bought the lady a drink. There was a group playing on a little stage in the pub and his dad sang along to all the old songs.

During the afternoon they went for a walk in the park. They sat on a bench near the pond and watched a couple of kids feeding the ducks. From behind, their mother looked so like his mum that Buddy couldn't help pointing it out to his dad.

'Yeah, a bit,' his dad said then changed the subject quickly. ''Ere, I'm gonna get me 'arley back this week. I've been down the shop and I'm gonna pick it up on Saturday. Might buy you an 'elmet while I'm about it – how'd you fancy that?'

Buddy said it would be great and his dad started telling him stories about the old days when he used to drive along the coast with a gang of his mates. The stories were funny but Buddy felt that his dad was only telling them so that they wouldn't say anything more about his mum.

They had hamburgers and chips at a restaurant which was decorated like a cowboy saloon. The waiters all wore Stetson hats and had toy guns in their holsters. They both had a hard job keeping a straight face while they ordered their meal. When they finished eating, his dad suggested going to see a film.

'Aren't you going out?' Buddy asked, praying that the answer would be no.

'What, and 'ave you scream the street down again? No, ain't doing nothing for a bit. So, what do you fancy? A horror film? I know you love 'em.'

They finally decided on a Clint Eastwood film. It was all about a man who escaped from a prison on an island. It was really exciting to see how the escape was planned but Buddy couldn't help wishing they'd chosen another film.

They were both very quiet afterwards. All the way home, Buddy kept wanting to say, 'You won't get into any trouble, will you?' Several times he dared himself to say it when he'd counted to ten but each time his nerve failed him.

Just as they were going through the front door, Buddy turned and thought he saw a figure standing in the shadows across the road. He closed the door quickly and felt a shiver run down his spine. Who was it? The Beast? Could he have found out where he lived? But why would he come? Thank goodness his dad was staying in.

He went upstairs and stood on the edge of the bath to look out of the little window. The street was empty and he told himself not to start imagining stupid things or he'd have nightmares again.

He made some coffee and he and his dad sat in the front room drinking it. Buddy drew the curtains to make sure nobody could look in.

'What d'you reckon about getting the telly back, now I've got a bit of cash?'

'I don't mind.' Buddy thought of all the money they'd spent today and of how much it would cost to get the Harley-Davidson back. 'I thought you were saving up to buy another shop.'

'I said "maybe". I don't know yet, do I?'

'You'll never do it if you spend it all.'

'Oh, turn it up. It's my money, right? I'll do what I want with it.'

Buddy could've kicked himself. As usual, he'd tried to say something and it had come out all wrong, and now his dad was annoyed.

They finished their coffee in silence and Buddy went to bed feeling miserable – he'd spoiled a good day.

# Chapter Thirteen

'Clark,' Mr Normington said after registration on Monday morning, 'I was checking the reply slips for the consultation evening and I noticed that I haven't had one from your parents. I trust you delivered it.'

'Yes, sir,' he lied. He'd forgotten all about it.

'Well? Are they coming? As I remember, it's usually your mother, is it not?'

'Yes, sir, but she can't come this time.'

'Your father is coming instead, I take it?'

'I'm not sure, sir. He might be working.'

Mr Normington tutted and raised his eyebrows. 'Is he, or is he not working? I've allocated fifteen minutes for each consultation and I don't wish to juggle with the times at this late stage.'

Buddy panicked and said, 'I'm sure he'll be able to come.'

'Good. I would be pleased if you would confirm that, first thing tomorrow.'

It took Buddy nearly all evening to pluck up the courage to speak to his dad.

'A parents' what?'

'Consultation evening. On Friday.'

'What they want me for? You in trouble?'

'No. All the parents go. They just say how I've been getting on in all the subjects.'

'What's the matter with reports? That's what we used to 'ave at my school.'

'I wish they still had them.'

'I've never 'ad to go before.'

'Mum always used to go. It's nothing, honest. We just sit down and they say what I've done in the term.'

'We? Are you there an' all?'

'Of course I am – it's about me, isn't it?'

'Sounds daft to me. What time Friday?'

'Seven fifteen.'

'Well, I might manage it, I suppose. I'll 'ave to go straight off after.'

His dad signed the reply slip and Buddy didn't know whether he was pleased or not. He'd half hoped that his dad would say no and make up a good excuse. The thought of sitting there while his dad made all kinds of mistakes in front of Mr Normington was awful. On the other hand, he was glad that he didn't have to tell Mr Normington that nobody was coming.

Buddy grew more tense as Friday drew near. He asked around casually to find the times of other people's consultations and was relieved to discover that the parents of the worst snobs were due much later in the evening. Luckily, the twins' parents were due at seven thirty and since they had two children to talk about the next consultation wasn't until eight. With any luck, his dad wouldn't meet anyone except, perhaps, the Rybeeros. That wouldn't be too bad. He hated himself for thinking like that but he could never be sure that his dad wouldn't do or say something really embarrassing.

He felt less anxious about it, though, when last thing on Friday, Julius said, 'I hate these consultations – I just sit there hoping my dad won't say anything stupid. Last year he kept talking about ECGs instead of GCEs. I thought I was going to die.'

Buddy thought he was going to die when his dad came downstairs ready to go at six thirty. He was dressed in his complete Teddy boy outfit – drainpipe trousers, drape jacket with velvet collar, bootlace tie, thick crepe-soled shoes and fluorescent green socks. His hair was slicked back with oil and it was obvious that he'd taken great care to look as tidy as possible. He'd dressed himself in his 'best' for the occasion.

'I thought you had to go straight out afterwards,' Buddy said, not daring to come to the point but hoping his dad might change his mind and put on something else. Jeans – anything would be better than this.

'I am. Got me other stuff in 'ere,' he said, holding up a Woolworth's plastic bag.

Buddy's stomach turned to water and he felt sick. The evening was going to be a disaster. 'Dad,' he said weakly.

'What?'

'Can't you put something else on?'

'Why?'

'Well, it's just . . . Mr Normington . . . won't like it.'

'He'll 'ave to lump it then, won't he?' There was defiance in his dad's voice but a touch of sadness, too, and Buddy knew he'd hurt him.

The walk to school seemed to take ages. His dad was right. What did it matter what Mr Normington thought? It wasn't as if his dad looked scruffy or dirty – he looked really smart. But he did look different. Even some of the people in the street looked twice as they walked past.

They arrived at the school just after ten past seven. There were pupils and parents all over the school and Buddy led the way to his classroom feeling as if everyone was looking at him. He tried to stay a couple of steps ahead of his dad – not too far to let his dad know it, but enough so that people couldn't be sure they were together.

There were some chairs outside the classroom and his dad sat down while Buddy peeped through the window into the room. Colin Franks was sitting with his well-dressed parents talking to Mr Normington, who was wearing a dark suit with a small red rosebud in the buttonhole.

'It's not bad 'ere, is it?' his dad said and Buddy noticed that he was playing with the plastic bag and looking up and down the corridor, almost as if he were nervous. Buddy watched out of the corner of his eye as his dad brushed the collar of his jacket and touched the edges of his hair to make sure that it was still tidy. He wiped his hands on his trousers and then checked his nails.

'What's this Mr Normington like, then? All right, is he?'

That did it. His dad was scared. Mr Normington would have to lump it. He loved his dad and he didn't care who knew it. He sat down beside him and began telling him about the new block they were in – when it was built, the number of rooms, how they'd found cracks in the ceiling already – anything to stop his dad being scared.

The door opened and the Franks family came out and walked off down the corridor without even glancing in the direction of Buddy and his dad.

'Next, please,' Mr Normington called.

Buddy took a deep breath and led the way in.

Mr Normington was standing behind the desk. Buddy saw the eyebrows flicker and the smile freeze as he caught sight of his dad's clothes. There was a brief silence then Mr Normington pulled himself together.

'Ah, Mr Clark. How do you do?' He held his hand out and Buddy's dad went to shake it with the hand holding the plastic bag. He laughed nervously, put the bag down on Mr Normington's desk then shook hands.

'Pleased to meet you.'

'Yes, well . . . Do sit down, Mr Clark, and you, Buddy. Right, where shall we begin? The reports first, perhaps. Oh.' Mr Normington found that all his papers were under the plastic bag. Buddy leaped up and pulled the bag away and Mr Normington began reading the comments that each of the teachers had made. Buddy was so tense that he barely listened, though he was dimly aware that they all sounded quite good. After every subject report Mr Normington stopped and looked at Buddy's dad who kept saying, 'Oh – nice.'

'Well,' Mr Normington said, pushing aside the reports, 'as you can see from those comments, Buddy is doing very well in 3E. We're very pleased with him.'

'Oh – nice.'

'Of course, it's a long way off yet, but we're hoping for great things from him in GCEs.'

'Oh – nice.'

'Have you talked about careers yet?'

Buddy's dad glanced at him with a slightly worried look, so Buddy butted in, 'Well, we've talked about some things but I haven't made up my mind yet.'

'Of course. I'm sorry, Mr Clark,' Mr Normington said, looking down at Buddy's record card, 'I can't recall what you do for a living.'

Buddy's heart raced.

'Ah, yes – here it is. Oh, you worked at Bradley's. That's closed down, hasn't it?'

'Yeah, beginning of the year. I do a bit with antiques on the side now. I'm 'oping to start a shop like what I used to 'ave.'

Buddy winced at the dropped 'h's but Mr Normington nodded and smiled.

'Well, then,' he said, 'I don't think there's much else from our end. Unless, of course, you've got any problems at your end?'

'No, everyfink's fine,' his dad said quickly.

'Good. Good. Well, let's hope young Buddy keeps up the good work. Make sure you always supervise his prep, etcetera.'

'Prep?' his dad said, and darted a look at Buddy.

'Yes, private studies – in the evenings,' Mr Normington said.

'Oh, 'omework. Oh yes, he's good like that – always does it.'

'Not too much time wasted in front of the television?'

'We 'aven't got a telly. We . . . er . . . got rid of it.'

'Did you?' Mr Normington said, and Buddy could see he was impressed. 'Good. There's some splendid stuff on it, of course – but it can be a dreadful time-waster. Well, well – thank you for coming, Mr Clark.'

They all stood up and Buddy's dad shook hands with Mr Normington.

'By the way, how's Mrs Clark? Well, I trust.'

'Oh, yeah – she's OK.'

'Good. Give her my regards.'

'Yeah, I will.'

As they walked to the door, Buddy could almost feel the relief pouring off his dad.

Julius and Charmian were waiting outside with their parents. They all stood up and Buddy said, 'Hello. This is my dad.' There was more shaking of hands and Buddy prayed that his dad wouldn't say anything horrible about black people. He needn't have worried. His dad was so obviously glad that the interview was over that he was smiling as if they were old friends.

'How'd it go?' Charmian whispered.

'It was OK.'

'Lucky you; we've still got ours,' Julius said and crossed his fingers.

The twins asked about his marks and what the teachers had said and by the time he'd finished telling them, his dad was deep in conversation with the Rybeeros.

'It bring back old times,' Mrs Rybeero was saying with a broad grin. She saw Buddy looking and said, 'You didn't tell us you dad like rock 'n' roll. An' my, him dress nice. Them was the days – Little Richard, Fats Domino.'

'Yeah, but Buddy Holly was the King,' his dad said. 'I saw 'im, you know – in '58 when 'e was over 'ere. Cor, 'e was brilliant. I mean, them others was good, too, but, I don't know, there was somefing about 'im – 'is voice an' all. It was like 'e was singing fings you knew about – know what I mean? Like fings that 'ad 'appened to you?'

Mrs Rybeero nodded enthusiastically and his dad's face was alive with pleasure at finding some people who shared his interest in rock 'n' roll. Buddy could see that he was ready to go on talking but there was a cough from behind them. Mr Normington was waiting in the doorway.

'Oh blimey – great start,' Julius groaned as his parents excused themselves for keeping Mr Normington waiting.

'They're all right, ain't they?' his dad said as they got outside. 'Funny they prefer the black singers like Fats and Little Richard. Still, they're all right. That Normington bloke's a bit of a berk, though, ain't 'e?'

Buddy could have hugged him.

They walked part of the way together then his dad said, 'Well, I'm off. You'll be OK goin' 'ome? And no screamin' the 'ouse down, right?' He went off towards the centre of town, swinging his plastic bag.

The journey home seemed to take no time at all. Buddy's body felt springy and he wanted to laugh and shout out as he thought how silly he'd been earlier.

He was whistling as he put the key in the front door and let himself in. The whistle died on his lips as he looked back across the road. Someone was standing in the shadows opposite the house in the same place that he'd thought he'd seen someone on Sunday. There was no doubt this time, though. It was real.

He dashed inside and slammed the door behind him then fumbled for the light switch. The light flashed on and he switched it off again and crept back to the door. He lifted the flap of the letterbox. The figure was still there, a darker shape in the darkness of the shadows.

## Chapter Fourteen

Buddy tiptoed through to the kitchen and checked that the back door was locked. He wondered whether to open it and slip away over the back gardens. And then what? Besides, it was nerve-racking at the best of times – dodging from hiding place to hiding place, scared of being seen by someone or of meeting a fierce dog. To do it now, in the dark, would be terrifying, especially if the Beast guessed what he was doing and followed. That would be a living nightmare – chased through the dark by the Beast.

If it was the Beast, of course. Who else could it be? The other man – what was his name? Mr King. No, it had to be the Beast. Yet, why? And how had he found out the address?

If only they hadn't taken the phone away. Perhaps he could open the door and yell for help. No – once the door was open, the Beast could stop him before anyone heard. He imagined himself being pushed back into the house with the Beast's hand clamped across his mouth. The safest thing was to stay locked inside and hope that he would go away.

He pulled open a drawer and fumbled round for a knife. He felt the edge of it and cursed – it was almost blunt. Still, better than nothing.

He went upstairs quietly – he might get a better view from the bathroom window. He stood on the edge of the bath and eased the little window open. He peered down, screwing his eyes up to concentrate on that patch of gloom. The figure had gone. He looked up and down the road but, as far as he could see, it was empty.

He was just stepping off the bath when the bell rang. He started with shock and slipped. The knife fell from his hand and clattered in the bath. He heard its metallic scrape as it slid from one side of the bath to the other then came to rest in the middle. There was a long silence as he lay on the floor, hardly daring to breathe.

The bell rang again. He leaped to his feet, groped for the knife and started downstairs. The sensible thing would be to go into the kitchen, ready to rush out the back door if the Beast tried to come in the front, but he found himself drawn towards the front door. It was as if it would be less scary if he could actually see outside.

How strange – not long ago it had been the Beast who'd been inside his house wondering who was knocking at the door. Perhaps this was just his revenge – to show Buddy how frightening it was. Perhaps he would now go away.

Buddy slowly lifted the flap of the letterbox until there was a small gap. He could see the collar of a coat and the white skin of the neck. The figure took a step backwards and the face came into view. He let go of the flap and stood up. His fingers trembled as he clawed at the latch but at last he turned it and jerked the door open.

'Hello, Buddy,' his mum said.

He didn't know what to do or say. He hadn't seen her for nearly six months – was he still allowed to hug her like the old days? He thought of shaking hands but that was ridiculous. He leaned against the door frame and swung the door wider so that she could come in, but she shook her head and glanced down the road as if she wanted to go. His heart sank. His mum wasn't coming home; she still hated him for stealing. She turned to him but he looked at the ground and began playing with the catch on the door.

'You don't seem very pleased to see me.' Her voice was accusing, almost angry.

He shrugged and flicked the catch a couple of times to cover up the silence.

'I'd better go, then.'

'You can come in if you want.' He tried to make it sound friendly but it came out as a mumble.

'No, I'd better go.'

Tears began to well up in his eyes and he pressed his thumb hard against the sharp edge of the catch to hurt himself.

'You're all right, are you?'

He nodded and clenched his teeth tightly to stop a tear from sliding out of his eye.

'Why are you all in the dark?'

He turned and looked into the house, pretending that he hadn't noticed that the lights were off.

'I thought you were someone else,' he said, keeping his face turned away.

'What?'

He repeated it, louder.

'Oh. You're not in trouble, are you?'

He shook his head and the first tear splashed against his nose as he did so.

'Sure?'

He nodded and kept staring towards the kitchen until he heard her shoes scrape on the doorstep as she started to walk away. He listened as her footsteps faded away, then closed the door and sat down on the bottom step of the stairs. When he leaned forward, the tears ran down his nose and splattered on to his shoes.

He rubbed his eyes fiercely with the sleeve of his pullover, glad that the rough texture made his skin sore. It was always the same. Whenever he started crying he found himself wishing that someone could see him. Like now – he wanted his mum to see him and feel sorry for him. Not even his tears were real.

Yes, he wanted her back. Well, then – wasn't that why he was crying? Partly. But there were other things, too. Why hadn't he told her he was sorry? Because he was a phoney – that's why. It was the same with his dad. If he really loved him, he wouldn't care what other people thought about him or the clothes he wore.

He was crying because he hated himself. He was crying because he was scared. And because he felt sorry for himself. And because all these feelings jumbled around inside him until he didn't know what was what.

How could he love his dad and be ashamed of him at the same time? How could he love his mum and hate her for leaving? Or want to be part of 3E and yet despise it? If he really thought stealing was wrong, why did he do it? Why couldn't he be simple, instead of having all these opposite things in him?

He stood up and went to the kitchen, bumping against the wall. He ran the cold water and splashed it on his face. He was drying himself on the towel when the bell rang. This time it probably was the Beast, but he didn't care.

He opened the door. It was his mum again.

'Buddy, I don't want to stay here in case your dad comes back. Come for a walk, will you? Please.'

They walked quickly, without talking, until they were well away from his road, then his mum slowed down. She asked if he knew where there was a café open and at least that gave them something to talk about. In the end, the nearest place they could think of was the snack bar at the bus station.

Buddy sat at a table in the corner while she went up to the counter. She came back with a Coke and a doughnut for him and a cup of tea for herself.

'You've cut your hair,' he said.

She smiled and patted the short strands that barely covered her ears. 'Do you like it?'

He nodded but it wasn't true – he preferred it when it used to come down to her shoulders. One of the pictures he'd had in his mind all this time was the way she always had to sweep it away from her face when she bent down to do something. Other things were changed, too. She was thinner and she wasn't wearing any make-up.

He took a bite of the doughnut but it was stale. His mouth was dry and it took ages to chew it. Would she be angry if he left it? Suddenly, he wished he hadn't come. He felt awkward and nervous. He took a sip of his drink to help him swallow the cake.

'You haven't half grown,' she said.

'Have I?'

'Nearly taller than me.'

He picked up the salt cellar, poured some salt on the shiny black surface of the table and began making patterns in it with his finger. This was terrible. If he didn't say it now, he'd never be able to. They'd go on saying silly things and it would be too late.

He pushed the salt into a pile then put his finger in the middle and moved it round to make a big 'O'. Without looking up, he said it – 'I'm sorry.'

'What?'

'I'm sorry.' His finger trembled and broke the circle of salt. 'About that money.'

'What money?'

He looked up. She didn't know what he was talking about. There was a puzzled frown on her face.

'I thought . . .'

'What, my love. Tell me.'

She didn't hate him. He could see it in her eyes. And she'd called him 'her love'.

'I thought you went away because I stole the money from your purse.'

She put her hand to her mouth and closed her eyes. She stayed like that, shaking her head, until he began to be worried. He looked round. Nobody was watching. He reached across and touched her other hand. Her fingers gripped him tight.

'Buddy, it's not true. You mustn't ever think it. Promise me. Never think it, never say it. It's not true. Promise me.'

'I promise.'

She let go of his hand and glanced round the café then edged her chair nearer the table.

'I had to get away, Buddy. Not because of you. Not even just because of your dad. For me, I suppose. It's hard to explain. I still love you, though. Both of you.'

Buddy suddenly remembered his dad hiding the photo. They still loved each other. It had all been a mistake. Everything could be all right again.

'Will you come home?' he asked.

'I can't – not just like that.'

'Why?'

She shook her head and twisted her cup round and round in the saucer.

'I can't, that's all.'

'Do you love someone else?'

'No, no, it's not that. Oh, Buddy – can you understand? I want to come home but at the same time I don't.'

She stopped, as if she was sure he couldn't make any sense out of what she was saying, but he could. It was something he knew only too well.

'Lots of times I nearly came back. Last Sunday I went round to the house. I saw you with your dad and all I wanted to do was come in and see you both – talk to you. But I knew it wouldn't be any good. It would all be the same like before. And I can't . . . go through all that again. I'm selfish, that's what it is. I want you – but changed, different. Not you. Your dad. Our life. Not all the rows again. We got married too young, had you too young. I missed out on everything. I'm not a very good mum.'

'You are. Mum, don't say that – you are.' He'd blurted it out too loud and he could see by the way that his mum's eyes flicked round the room that people must be listening. He fought back the tears. He would not cry. He would not.

'Here, I'm going to school now. Well, not school – evening classes. Business Studies. Three evenings a week. Can you imagine me scribbling away at a desk? We learn all about computers and things. I'm a right dunce,' she laughed.

'I bet you're not.'

'If I pass the exams I'm going to get a better job. Same company but more responsibility, better money.' She lowered her voice again. 'Is your dad working?'

Buddy shook his head – he mustn't tell her about that. 'He might get a job driving taxis. They need drivers.'

His mum's mouth tried to smile but couldn't.

'Let's go,' she said, standing up. He waited at the door while she went to the counter and paid.

They walked back slowly and she told him about the flat she shared with a lady from her office. He only half listened because he was going over and over in his mind what he wanted to say.

'I've written the address,' she said, stopping and fumbling with her bag. She handed him a piece of paper. 'If you want, you can come round and see me – any time. Buddy, you mustn't hate me for what I've done.'

'I don't. I love you.'

She bit her lip and fumbled with her bag again.

'Look, I won't come any further. Here's some money. No, please take it. Buddy, please.'

He took the money and bundled it into his pocket with her address. Now. He had to say it now, before she went. It burst out of him – all in the wrong order.

'Dad loves you. He's going to save up and buy a shop again. He's going to get a job. He looks at your photo. Honest, I know he loves you. He wants you to come home. So do I.' His voice was trembling and the breath was bursting his lungs.

'I can't. Not yet. I'll think about it. I promise.' She walked away a couple of steps then stopped. 'Come and see me. Don't say anything to your dad. Just give me time. Buddy?'

He nodded and she went, turning once to wave before she disappeared round the corner.

He walked slowly, but speeded up as the thought struck him – she only wanted a bit of time to think. He started to trot. She was going to think it over. And if he could prove that his dad had changed, she'd come back. That was obvious. She still loved them. He was running now, the wind making his eyes water and his throat raw with the cold. Somehow or other he'd make his dad get a proper job – driving a taxi, anything. And when his mum saw how things had changed, she would come back. She would.

## Chapter Fifteen

The whole thing didn't seem so easy the next morning. For a start, his dad talked of nothing else but the Harley-Davidson. He'd arranged to pick it up at two that afternoon and, as promised, he was going to buy a helmet for Buddy. He talked so excitedly about it that Buddy didn't have the heart to bring up the subject of a job. It would only cause a row.

When they got to the bike shop, the Harley-Davidson was outside, polished and all ready to go. His dad ran his hand over the handlebars before they went in. They were met by the man who had taken it away on the truck. This time, though, he was all smiles and friendly chat as the papers were signed and the money was handed over.

'We've looked after it nicely for you. I knew it would only be temporary like. We all run short sometimes.' He beamed.

'See what a bit of money does,' his dad said as the man hurried off to get a selection of helmets to show them.

Buddy had just been thinking the same thing and he knew it would make his task even harder – his dad would hardly want to work as a taxi driver when he was making so much money already.

The shopkeeper tried to persuade him to buy a really expensive helmet but Buddy deliberately chose the cheapest. It wasn't very comfortable and it looked awful but at least it would mean that there was a bit more to go towards the record shop. Though, more and more, he was beginning to think that the shop was just a wild dream.

They drove fast through the town and even faster when they got on to the dual carriageway along the coast. Normally, Buddy would have found it exciting but he wasn't in the mood.

'Slow down,' he shouted as they weaved in and out of the traffic too fast. Cars hooted at them but his dad just laughed and accelerated so that all Buddy could do was move closer to his back and hang on tight.

They stayed on the main road for about twenty minutes then turned on to a side road that twisted and climbed towards the cliffs. The tyres screamed as they skidded and slid around the corners overlooking the steep drops to the sea. When they reached the highest point, his dad twisted the handlebars and they bounced off the road on to the grass of the clifftop. For one terrible instant Buddy thought they were going over the edge but at the last moment they swerved away and stopped.

Buddy stumbled off, shaking with fright and cold, his hands numb from the wind. 'You're mad! We could've had a crash.'

'Chick, chick, chick, chicken,' his dad teased.

'I don't care – you're stupid.'

'Nah, it's great. Gotta take a few risks.'

'Yeah, it's all right for you.' Buddy's anger blazed and he lashed out hard at his dad's arm.

''Ere, do that again and I'll knock your block off.'

Buddy avoided the blow that his dad aimed at his shoulder and ran across the grass towards the road. He turned left and headed back the way they'd come. It was all downhill and he ran fast, his weight carrying him almost too quickly for his legs, the shock of each step rattling his teeth. Halfway down, there was a roar and the bike shot past. It rounded a corner and the noise of the engine faded away.

He slowed to a walk and felt in his pocket for the money his mum had given him. At least he could catch a bus home – if there were any buses. Better than going back on the bike. His dad was mad and reckless. No wonder his mum had walked out on him. He was crazy and selfish – he just didn't care about how anyone else felt. Let him drive fast and kill himself. Let him get into trouble with the police. It would serve him right.

When he reached the bottom of the hill he rounded the final bend and found his dad sitting at the side of the road next to the bike. Buddy was going to walk right past but his dad stood up and grinned shyly.

'OK. I'm stupid. I'm sorry.' He knocked with his knuckles on the top of Buddy's helmet. 'My nut's as thick as that. Come on – don't be angry.' Then he pulled such a silly face that Buddy couldn't help laughing.

His dad drove slowly and carefully along the narrow road that ran near the sea. They stopped and walked on the beach for a while then went to a small café for a drink. There was a pinball table and his dad challenged him to a game. Buddy won the first game but his dad said it was only because he couldn't play properly without music.

'That's better,' he said as he fed some coins into the jukebox and the music boomed out. 'Now, I'll show you who's king.'

His dad won five games in a row and Buddy had to admit he was good.

'Course I'm good. I've 'ad the training, ain't I? All them years down Rube's caff when I shoulda been in school. Mind, I'd rather be a genius like you – and I ain't kidding, neither.'

It was dark when they got back to town. His dad dropped him at home and said he'd probably be late back. Buddy wanted to say something about the rotten hours his dad worked and then try and lead on to the whole thing about the job, but the bike roared away before he could bring himself to start talking.

The time passed incredibly slowly. Buddy was bored and lonely. He tried reading but he couldn't settle to it. His mind was buzzing. If only his dad would start the record shop again, he could tell his mum everything was all right.

At nine o'clock he decided to walk into the centre of town. He would have liked to go and visit his mum – she'd said come any time – but there was nothing good to tell her yet. There was a road map outside the town hall; at least he could go and find out where the road was. He took the piece of paper from his back pocket and looked at the address – 23b Raynall Avenue.

It was drizzling slightly when he reached the town hall and he had to wipe the glass to see the map. There was a key to the roads at the bottom. Raynall Avenue was in square E5. The street lights reflected on the glass and made it hard to see but in the end he found it. He traced the shortest way to get there from his house and thought about how one day he would make that journey with his dad to pick up his mum's things and bring her home.

He wondered about whether to go round there now – just to see the house – but the drizzle was turning to rain and his sweater was already damp. As he started for home, there was the far-off sound of a siren. It grew louder and louder until a police car came racing towards him with its blue light flashing.

Instinctively, Buddy stepped back into a shop doorway until it passed then began to run through the rain which was now pelting down. The drops stung his face and trickled down his neck. The rain eased as he turned into his road and it stopped completely just as he reached his front door, but he was already soaked.

He ran a hot bath and lay in it, feeling it drive the cold from his body and relax him. By the time he'd dried himself, he could barely keep his eyes open. It was ten thirty. His dad might be home soon. He got into bed and tried to read to keep awake but it was no good. He switched off the light and closed his eyes.

'Buddy!'

His dad was calling him and it was part of his dream but it was real, too. Perhaps it was already morning. He opened his eyes and it was dark.

'Buddy!'

The voice was muffled. Where was he? Not in the room. Not in the corridor. He got out of bed and stumbled to the door. He switched on the corridor light and squinted in the sudden brightness. He pushed open the door to his dad's bedroom but the bed was empty.

'Dad?'

'In 'ere.' His voice was coming from the bathroom. Buddy went to push the door and then saw the blood. It had splashed round the door handle and run in long lines down the white paint.

'Buddy, don't come in. Stay there. Now, listen – I'm bleeding, right?'

'Dad!'

'Now, don't panic. Me 'ands are all cut but it's nuffin' – just blood. But I need you to 'elp me, see. There's some towels in the airing cupboard – I need 'em.'

Buddy ran and got a pile of towels from the cupboard. His hands were trembling and he was starting to feel weak. There were drops of blood all the way up the stairs and along the corridor.

'I've got them.'

'OK. Now, listen – don't you be silly, Buddy.'

'I won't.'

The door handle was slippery with blood and Buddy's knees wobbled as he opened the door. His dad was sitting on the edge of the bath. Buddy saw a pool of blood on the lino and then jerked his eyes away. He would concentrate on his dad's face. It was pale and damp and there was a glazed look in his eyes.

'Dad, what happened?'

'I thought I could do it on me own but I can't. I've got to wash me 'ands. There's a little bottle of disinfectant in that cabinet. Pour some in the sink then fill it up wiv water and rinse it round. It's gotta be clean. Right. Now put the plug back in and fill the sink wiv water again. Good. Now pour a lot of disinfectant in. More. That'll do.'

Buddy did as he was told, following each instruction quickly but calmly. He watched the water go cloudy as the disinfectant mixed with it. So far it had been easy – the hard part was coming.

'You'll 'ave to 'elp me off wiv me jacket. And me shirt.'

His dad stood up and swayed slightly. Buddy could hear the blood dripping on to the lino but he didn't look down. He worked fast, unzipping the leather jacket and easing it off his dad's shoulders and down his arms. He saw a blur of red as the hands slipped out of the end of the sleeves. He slung the jacket over the rim of the bath and started undoing the front of his dad's shirt. Now for the buttons on the sleeves. The cuffs were soaked with blood. Buddy gritted his teeth and undid the buttons quickly.

'Good lad,' his dad said as Buddy pulled the shirt off. 'Now, just 'old on to me, will you? I'm gonna put me 'ands in the water and it's gonna 'urt like mad. I don't want to go falling and banging me nut on the bath.'

Buddy stood behind him and put his hands on his shoulders. There was a moment's hesitation then his dad leaned forward and put his hands in the water. He gasped and moaned. His whole body went rigid with the pain. Buddy gripped the shoulders and felt the muscles, tight and knotted with the effort.

Gradually, the muscles relaxed and his dad sighed. 'Blimey, it don't 'alf sting. OK – you can let go now.'

'Shall I call the doctor or something?'

'No.'

'Maybe you need stitches.'

'No.'

'What happened?'

'I come off the bike, didn't I?'

Buddy knew it was a lie, and he knew why his dad didn't want to see a doctor. He was in trouble.

'Dad, please.'

'Stop fussin' and get some towels. I want you to tie 'em round me 'ands.'

Buddy picked up a towel and held it ready. His dad pulled one hand out of the red water and Buddy wrapped the towel round it quickly.

'That's it. Tie it tight. Tighter.'

Buddy wound the towel as tight as he could then got another one and wrapped it round once and tied it. His dad lifted his other hand out of the water and this time Buddy caught sight of the deep cuts that criss-crossed the fingers and palm and stretched right up to the wrist. He drew back for a second then forced himself to wind the towel round. He got another towel and tied it round the wrist the first one hadn't covered.

His dad was shaking by the time he finished and his face was very pale. He put an arm round Buddy's shoulder and they walked slowly to his bedroom. He sat on the bed and Buddy bent down and took off his shoes.

'That's better,' his dad said as he lay down. Buddy covered him with the sleeping bag, tucking it up to his chin but leaving his arms outside. The blood was already beginning to seep through the towels so Buddy got a couple more and laid them under his dad's hands.

'That'll do. I'm OK. Listen, slip your jeans on and bring the 'arley round the back. Put it in the garden. I don't want no one to see it. And, Buddy, if anybody asks – I was 'ere all evening, right?'

He dashed into his room, got his jeans on and ran outside. The Harley was lying on the pavement. He glanced up and down the empty street then picked it up and wheeled it into the back garden. Back in the house he got another towel and started to clear up the mess in the bathroom. He'd just finished wiping the floor when he noticed a briefcase behind the door. He flicked the catch but it was locked. He shook it and there was a dull rattle.

'Buddy!' He dropped the case in shock and saw his dad in the doorway. 'Leave it alone.'

'What is it?'

'Nuffin'.'

He felt his temper rise. 'OK then, I'll put it in the dustbin.'

His dad sighed helplessly. 'OK – it's jewellery. And it don't need you knockin' it about.'

'Where'd you get it?'

'From a man.'

'You stole it, didn't you?'

'No, I did not. I told you – I'm buying and selling antiques.'

'Then how did you cut yourself?'

'I fell off me bike.'

'Like hell you did.'

His dad's eyes blazed. 'Shut up and go to bed. Go on.'

Buddy knew there was no point in talking – besides, his dad was weak and beginning to sway again. He walked out of the bathroom and into his room, took off his jeans and got into bed. A couple of minutes later, the hall light went off and he heard his dad groan as he lay down on his bed.

Well, he'd finally got the proof – as if he needed it. His dad *was* stealing. Even if he got away with it this time, it wouldn't be long before he was caught. That would be the end of everything. His mum would never come home. And what would happen to *him*, if his dad went to prison?

He buried his face in the pillow so his dad wouldn't hear him crying. He hated him.

# Chapter Sixteen

His dad got up early. Buddy heard him go downstairs and into the kitchen. There was the sound of running water then a clatter as something, probably the kettle, fell into the sink. He must be trying to make a cup of tea. A couple of minutes later there was another crash and his dad swore. He'd broken a cup. From the sounds, Buddy could picture the struggle as his dad tried to make the tea with his hands still wrapped in the towels.

He hoped his dad would call so he'd have the pleasure of pretending that he was still asleep. Let him struggle. Let him hurt his hands and make them bleed. He was a liar and a thief and he was ruining everything. All he cared about was his stupid bike. A proper dad wouldn't waste his money on things like that. A proper dad would have done everything he could to get an honest job and save his money and try to make his mum come home.

Buddy lay there letting his resentment build up but, gradually, the silence began to worry him. Suppose he'd fainted? The silence went on and on and finally he had to get up and see what had happened.

His dad was sitting at the kitchen table. His face seemed even whiter in the daylight and there were dark rings round his eyes. He'd roughly wrapped some new towels round his hands and only a bit of blood had soaked through. There was a broken cup on the floor and tea leaves all over the draining board.

Neither of them spoke as Buddy boiled the kettle and made the tea. He poured a cup of tea for each of them and sat down. His dad twice tried to lift the cup with his two fists but the tea slopped over the towels and he had to put it down again. Buddy took the cup and held it to his dad's lips while he drank.

'Bloomin' baby,' his dad mumbled and then grinned and said, 'You'll 'ave to change me nappy next.'

Buddy didn't laugh. It wasn't the time for jokes. 'You've got to stop it, Dad.'

'Stop what?'

'You know what. Stealing.'

'I told you . . .'

'I don't care what you told me. I know.'

'You don't know nuffin'.'

'Anything! Anything! You can't even talk properly.'

His dad got up, knocking his chair flying, and stamped out of the room.

'You don't care about me!' Buddy yelled as he went. 'You'll get into trouble and go to prison and then what?'

'Then you won't 'ave to put up wiv me,' his dad shouted back and went into the front room, kicking the door to behind him.

Buddy went upstairs and took his school things out of his bag – the bag his dad's money had paid for, just as it had paid for his trousers. So what? That's what dads were supposed to do, pay for things you had to have. Why should he feel grateful for that? Anyway, they were like stolen goods – he could probably be in trouble for accepting them. That was nothing to thank his dad for.

He opened his books and tried to do his homework but it was no good. He should never have lost his temper over a word his dad said wrong – that was just a waste of time when there were such important things to talk about. And now, when his dad needed him to help, was the best time to do it instead of sulking up here.

His dad was sitting on the sofa with his hands on his knees. He'd unwrapped the towels and laid them on his lap to stop the blood running on to his trousers. The cuts on the fingers and wrists had stopped bleeding but the deep gashes on his palms still oozed steadily.

'You ought to go to hospital,' Buddy said.

'I don't need none of your advice,' his dad said, flapping the ends of the towels over to hide his hands.

Buddy went to the window and stared out.

'I want you to ring someone.'

'What for?' Buddy asked, without turning round.

'None of your business.'

'I won't do it, then.'

'I thought you didn't want me to get in trouble.'

'I don't.'

'Well then? Look, I can't do it meself, can I? I want someone to come and get that bag, if you must know. It's too dangerous to keep it 'ere.'

'Why? It's because it's stolen, isn't it?'

'Yes, all right – it's stolen. Now are you satisfied?'

It was pointless crying but he couldn't help it. He slid down the wall on to the floor and the sobs shook his whole body. His dad came over and crouched down next to him, his hands bleeding.

'Don't do that, Buddy. Come on, stop crying.'

But he couldn't. He pulled his knees up to his face and shuddered with the misery that poured out of him. He thought he would never stop but, eventually, he cried himself out until only the occasional sob shook him.

'Crying don't help,' his dad said. 'Just makes it worse.'

'Can't be worse,' Buddy said and he started to hiccup

'You're joking. Being caught's worse.'

'Don't do it, then.'

'It ain't that easy. Once you start . . .'

'Course it is. I stopped nicking from shops.' His dad looked shocked and Buddy almost laughed but a hiccup came instead.

'I stopped.'

'I 'ope you did.' Then his dad realized. He shook his head and laughed. 'I'm a fine one to talk. Blimey, what a pair.'

'I stopped; you can.'

'You don't understand. I'm in too deep. It's not like nicking from shops.'

His dad got up and went back to the sofa. He dabbed his hands on the towels and then lay back with a sigh, staring at the ceiling. Buddy wiped his face and shifted his weight. His legs were numb and he was cold but, strangely, he felt happier. At least his dad was telling the truth now, and it was good to have been able to say about the shoplifting.

'I'll ring if you like,' he said.

His dad continued to stare at the ceiling and Buddy could see his Adam's apple moving up and down as if he had to keep on swallowing.

'Ta,' his dad said, at last.

'What's the number?'

'30065. Ask for a bloke called King. Tell 'im somefing went wrong and I want to see 'im at my place. Say it's urgent.'

Buddy memorized the number and got up and went to the door.

'Buddy!'

'What?'

'I'll try, all right?'

He was so excited about what his dad had said that it wasn't until he was dialling the number that he realized. King. Mr King – that was the name that the Beast had said. It was all beginning to come together.

The pips went and he pushed the coin into the slot.

'Hello,' said a voice.

'Can I speak to Mr King, please?'

'Speaking.'

Buddy gave the message. The man hesitated for a bit and sounded angry but he said he'd be over as soon as he could.

When he got home, his dad asked him to go to the Indian grocer's shop on the corner of Priory Street to see if they sold bandages. The lady there spent ages searching through the crowded shelves. She kept saying, 'I know we have them. I'm sure we have them,' and in the end she found them and he bought six packets.

'Ace!' his dad said when Buddy finished wrapping the bandages round. He'd done them really tight to try to press some of the big cuts together. His dad ought to have them stitched, but there was no point in saying anything.

Buddy spent the rest of the morning selecting records and playing them for his dad, who lay on the sofa with his arms above his head to try and stop the bleeding. Just after one o'clock, the bell rang and Buddy went to the door.

There was no doubt that Mr King was the man who'd taken the Rybeero taxi from outside number 56 – he fitted Julius's description perfectly. He was very short and fat. His white hair was quite long and his fringe touched the top of his thick glasses. The lenses magnified his eyes so that they looked too big for his face and he reeked of cigars.

'Terry's boy,' he said and patted Buddy on the cheek. 'What's your name – Tubby, isn't it?'

'Buddy.'

'That's right. Your dad in?'

Buddy showed him into the front room where his dad was standing up, looking rather anxious. His hands were thrust deep into the pockets of his trousers.

''Ello, . . . Des. Fanks for coming and that. Turn the music off, Buddy.'

'Just been talking to him,' Mr King said, patting Buddy's cheek again as he walked by to the record player. 'What you done to his hair?'

'Ain't me,' his dad said. 'They all got it, round 'ere. Skin'eads or somefing. 'Orrible, ain't it?'

'He's tall, too. Looks a right villain. How old is he?'

'Twelve.'

'I'm fourteen next week,' Buddy said. 'And I'm not a skinhead.'

'Fourteen,' Mr King said, sitting down in a chair without being asked. 'He shouldn't be that tall, should he? Not at fourteen. Anyway – um – has he got something to do?'

'Oh yeah – 'omework. 'E's a right brainbox at school. You'd better get on wiv it then, eh, Buddy? Upstairs.'

Buddy left the room and pulled the door to, deliberately not closing it fully. He stamped on the stairs on the way up then took off his shoes and tiptoed down again. He stood close to the door, ready to dash along to the kitchen if necessary.

Mr King was talking and his voice had lost all of its friendliness. It was hard and cold. 'I don't care what happened. I set up a safe house and it's your job to get it there. I take enough risks without having to worry about your end of things. You could have sent it round with that kid of yours.'

'No.'

'I'm not pleased, Terry. Don't let it happen again.'

There was a pause then his dad said quietly, 'I was finking maybe I ought to lay off it a bit.'

'A few days until your hands are better, but I've got a couple of jobs marked out for the weekend that've got to be done.'

'I don't know, Des.'

'Don't know what?'

'I fink I've 'ad enough.'

'Now look, Terry, I did you a favour letting you in on this.'

'I know but . . .'

'You owe me, so don't forget it. This isn't any of your small-time operations, you know; this is export stuff. I've got things running nice – customers in Europe and the States, and they expect delivery. So don't you start making life hard.'

'Des . . .'

'Don't "Des" me. I'm committed and so are you. You can have a few days off for your hands but I want you round Croxley Street at eight Friday evening. Understood? Good.'

Buddy tiptoed back up the stairs to his room. He was shaking with anger. Mr King had treated his dad like a little kid – his voice had been like Mr Normington's when he told someone off. And his dad had just taken it, too – he'd hardly said a thing. Why hadn't he hit him or kicked him out? So, now it would just go on as before. His dad would take more risks and, eventually, he would be caught – all because of that Mr King.

About five minutes later, his dad called him and Buddy went downstairs. His dad looked miserable but Mr King was smiling as if they'd only been having a friendly chat.

'Here he is,' Mr King said. 'What they call you at school – Beanpole?'

Buddy glared at him.

'I want a bag of some sort, big enough to hold this,' Mr King said, holding up the briefcase.

Buddy was furious at being ordered around by him, but at least it meant that he was taking the jewellery away. He found a large plastic bag in the kitchen and gave it to Mr King, who slipped the briefcase inside.

'Perfect. Well, I'll have to love you and leave you. Don't forget, Friday. No, stay there, Terry, and rest yourself. Long-shanks here can see me out.'

Buddy opened the front door. Mr King stepped out and began to turn as if to say goodbye but Buddy closed the door before he could speak.

He went into the kitchen and heated up some soup and made some toast. He didn't feel at all hungry but they ought to eat. He crumbled the toast into his dad's soup to make it easier but his dad still had trouble with the spoon. He'd eaten less than half of it when he threw down the spoon and went upstairs to bed. Not a word had been spoken.

Buddy sat in the front room brooding over all the terrible things that were likely to happen. The afternoon thickened towards dusk and the room grew gloomier. He decided to match his mood by making it even darker. He drew the curtains and then, as he was sitting down again, the idea came to him.

It was so shocking that he tried to push it out of his mind but it wouldn't go. It stayed there and grew until it seemed the only solution. He tried to tell himself it was wrong but the more he thought about the facts, the less wrong it seemed. Before he knew what was happening, he'd accepted the plan and was beginning to work out the details. One after the other, the pieces fell into place until only one doubt remained in his mind. He went up to his dad's room.

'Are you asleep, Dad?'

'No.'

'I got worried.'

'What about?'

'Supposing the police caught Mr King with that bag.'

'Don't worry about 'im – 'e's too sharp.'

'But supposing they did. Would he split on you?'

'Don't be daft. 'E's plenty of fings, but 'e ain't a grass.'

'Oh. You all right?'

'Yeah. I'll stay 'ere and try to kip a bit.'

'OK. Night.'

Buddy closed the door and went downstairs. That was it, then. The last problem had been solved.

The plan was complete.

## Chapter Seventeen

When Buddy got home from school the next day he helped his dad change his bandages. The bleeding had finally stopped and it was now possible to see how deep some of the cuts were. Buddy's head started to swim at one stage when he thought he saw the white of bone at the bottom of a long cut on a finger.

His dad swore a couple of times with the pain but he kept telling Buddy to tie the bandages tightly. When it was finished, he tried wiggling his fingers but a couple of them still weren't moving properly and he sat rubbing them gently. There was a worried expression on his face and Buddy felt guilty about leaving him alone but it had to be done.

'I've got to go out, Dad.'

'Oh, where?'

'Down the Satellite. We're painting it up and I said I'd help. Just for a few hours. I did my homework at school.' The lies were all prepared and they slipped out easily and convincingly. 'Don't know how long I'll be. Do you want anything?'

'Nah, I'll be all right. Oh yeah – you can make us a cuppa tea.'

Buddy cursed silently. It was already nearly five o'clock. He went into the kitchen and put the kettle on. It would take over twenty minutes to get to his mum's office. He mustn't miss her. The kettle seemed to take ages to boil and when it did he was so anxious to pour it quickly that some drops splashed round the rim of the teapot and burned his fingers.

'Right – see you,' he said when he took the tea in.

'You ain't goin' like that, are you? You'll get paint on your trousers.'

'Oh yeah, I forgot.'

He ran upstairs and changed quickly, leaving his school clothes dumped in a pile by his bed.

'Bye,' he shouted, dashing down and out of the front door before there were any more delays.

He ran all the way and it was just five thirty by the time he got to the office. He stood on the other side of the main road and watched the people coming out. The flow of people was so steady that the automatic doors never had time to close. He was worried in case his mum came out in a large group and he missed her.

At last, she came out of the doors, talking to two women. They stopped on the pavement smiling and chatting. His mum said something and one of the women laughed and touched his mum's arm. Buddy felt a strange swell in his heart. That was his mum. She had friends who laughed with her and liked her. She looked so smart, and it was true, her short hair really did suit her. The three of them talked for a moment longer then the other two said goodbye and walked away. His mum turned in the other direction. Buddy watched her go, then followed, keeping to his side of the road.

It gave him a thrill that she didn't know he was there, as if he were seeing something secret and hidden that brought him closer to her. No one else in the world was watching her stop at that shop and look in the window. Not even his dad or her friends from the office could see her change her bag from her left to her right shoulder then quickly pat the back of her hair. And everything was being done naturally, for herself alone – because she didn't know anyone was there.

For ten minutes he followed, watching her every move: the way her skirt swayed when she walked, how the collar of her jacket brushed the jagged line of her hair, how she rocked back on her heels while she was waiting to cross roads. He wished he could be invisible and watch her for days – at work, at her new home. He wanted to be inside her head – to know what she thought. How often did she think of him? Perhaps she was thinking of him now, as she waited at the traffic lights for a break in the stream of cars.

When she turned left down a quiet side road, he ran after her. She heard his footsteps and turned. There was a look of shock then she smiled. He wanted to hug her but he held himself back.

'Buddy! Fancy seeing you.'

'I was coming round to see you. You said come round.'

They looked at each other and Buddy suddenly felt awkward and clumsy. While he'd been following her, it had all seemed so easy but here, face to face, he didn't know what to say.

'Come on, then,' she said, and they started walking. 'How's school?'

'OK.'

He wanted to say something else – anything that would keep them talking – but he couldn't think of a single thing. The one thing that he wanted to say, the question he had to ask, burned in his head but he couldn't just come out with it.

He became aware of the sound of their footsteps. Twice he nearly asked her a question about work but the words wouldn't come out. He stepped on an uneven bit of pavement and their shoulders bumped so he moved further away from her. His jeans made a scraping sound as the legs brushed. He tried to stop it by keeping his legs further apart but he thought it must look strange so he went back to walking normally.

'Here we are,' she said. 'We're in the basement.'

Buddy didn't even look at the house. He wanted to run away, but he forced himself to follow her down the steps.

'I can never get this door open first time,' she said, fumbling with the key.

Buddy gave a silly sort of laugh, then wished he hadn't.

The next half hour seemed endless. He said the flat was nice and, 'Yes, please,' he would like a cup of tea, then he sat in silence while his mum got it ready. He'd just been on the point of forcing himself to say why he'd come, when the woman who shared the flat arrived home from work.

'This is Joyce,' his mum said.

He got up quickly and knocked the table so hard with his leg that the bottle of milk fell over. Milk ran everywhere and dripped on to the floor. The two women mopped it up while he stood, embarrassed, in a corner. Then they all sat at the table and drank their tea. His mum and Joyce started talking about work. They went on about some man who wouldn't let Joyce make important decisions. Twice, Joyce said she hoped that Buddy wouldn't grow up thinking that men were better than women. He shook his head and tried to look interested but he wished she would go away so that he could be alone with his mum. Every passing minute would make it harder to say.

At last, Joyce stood up and left, saying she had things to do in her room.

'What do you think of her?' his mum asked. 'Isn't she great?'

Buddy nodded.

'She's been fantastic to me – letting me share this place and everything. We just talk the whole time about everything – politics, books – things I never used to talk about. She's like a sister – you know what I mean?'

Buddy nodded but he felt sad and empty, as though Joyce was a sort of rival for his mum's love. He and his dad never talked about books and politics. How could they hope to win her back when she was so happy here?

'I like books,' he said.

His mum lit a cigarette. 'I'm trying to cut down,' she said, holding the cigarette up straight and looking at it. 'I hope you haven't started.'

He shook his head.

'Well, don't. I suppose your dad's still smoking those old roll-your-owns? I always think about him whenever I smell that smoke somewhere.' She smiled and did an imitation of the way his dad flicked a cigarette from one side of his mouth to the other.

Buddy laughed and then seized the opportunity. 'Will you come and see him on Friday?'

'Buddy, I can't.'

'Why not? Are you doing something?'

'No.'

'Well?'

'I just can't. It's not that easy. I don't know what I feel. I don't know what he feels.'

'He loves you. I know.'

'You can't be sure. I'm the one that left. He might not want me after that. Anyway, I don't know if I want – all that – again.'

She got up and walked over to the sink. She flicked some ash into it then suddenly turned on the tap and held the cigarette under the water before throwing it into the rubbish bin.

'You said you missed us,' Buddy said.

'I do. But it might be different when I'm back there. Supposing it doesn't work out? I don't want to do all this to you again. I'm a bad enough mum as it is.'

'You keep saying that, and it's not true.'

'Oh, Buddy, Buddy.'

'It doesn't mean you have to come back yet – just talk. Please.'

He could feel that she was nearly ready to say yes and he was suddenly scared. Supposing she was right? Supposing it was too soon for them to meet? It might ruin any chance that they would get together again. It would have been much better if he'd had more time to arrange things, talk to his dad and get him in the right mood. But he didn't have the time. He had to make sure that his dad didn't leave the house on Friday, and this was the only way he could think of doing it. And it wouldn't go wrong, mustn't go wrong.

'Please, Mum. Just talk – that's all. You'll see, everything's better now.'

She was still at the sink, looking out of the window at the brick wall below the garden. He got up and stood behind her. He could smell her perfume and he wanted to pull her close so she'd know how much he loved her.

'Go on, Mum. He'll be at home on Friday if you come at half past seven.'

She breathed deeply then nodded. 'All right. But no promises about anything. Understand?'

'Yes.'

Now the decision had been made, they both seemed to relax and it was easy to talk and laugh. She took out a photo from her bag and showed it to him. It was of him when he was eighteen months, standing next to her on a beach. They fell about laughing at how fat he looked and how young she looked in a tiny miniskirt, with her hair piled up on top of her head and her eyes plastered with mascara.

'I wasn't half mad when I was carrying you,' she said, 'because I was too big to wear my minis. Don't laugh, I loved my minis.'

He talked about school and she told him about her work and her evening classes. She got really excited when she spoke about the things she was learning and he loved to see the happiness on her face. It was a whole new side to her.

He would have liked to stay longer but he didn't want to be too late in case his dad became suspicious about where he'd been. He reminded her that she had to be there by seven thirty on Friday and she promised that she wouldn't be late.

As they stood at the front door, he realized how much he had grown – she had to turn her face up slightly to look at him now. She ran her hand over his hair and gave him a quick kiss on the cheek, then went back inside.

During the walk home, he told himself that it had gone well. The most difficult part was over. Now, all he had to do was arrange the other half of the plan with Charmian.

*

Seeing Charmian turned out to be harder than he'd expected. He'd forgotten that she did judo on Tuesdays at lunchtime, and during the other breaks she was always talking to somebody else. Finally, he had to write her a note during the last lesson, asking her to meet him alone in the library after school. He underlined 'alone', folded the note, and threw it across the aisle to her while the teacher's back was turned. Julius saw him do it and gave him a questioning look but Buddy ignored him.

At the end of the lesson, he went straight to the library. There were a few kids there choosing books but no one from 3E. He sat at a table and waited but after ten minutes he began to wonder if something had gone wrong so he went to the door. She was coming along the corridor and he ran to her.

'Sorry – Jules was being awkward. He wanted to come.'

'Did you tell him anything?'

'Only that I was seeing you. What's it all about, anyway?'

Buddy had thought about only telling her part of the plan and lying about why he was doing it, but in the end he'd decided that he must tell her the whole truth. He waited until they were out in the deserted playground and then began. It was hard at first – saying things that he'd tried to keep secret – but soon it was pouring out.

They stood in the empty bike sheds and Charmian listened without interrupting as he described how he'd discovered what his dad was doing. Then he went over his plan, step by step, telling her what he wanted her to do.

In the silence after he finished, he realized that, some time while he'd been talking, it had started to rain. It was beating on the corrugated iron roof of the shed and the cold wind was blowing some drops in on them. They moved further in and leaned against the back wall.

'I'm scared,' Charmian said.

'Why?'

'The police and everything – I don't like it. He'll go to jail, Buddy. Because of us.'

'Well, he's a thief, isn't he? My dad wants to stop, Char, and he won't let him. And what about Mrs Solomon? He's the one who's making her scared.'

He felt bad about using Mrs Solomon in the argument because he didn't care anything about her. On the other hand, he was desperate: without Charmian's help he'd never be able to do it. He went on and on about how horrible Mr King was and how he was ruining so many people's lives and he even hinted that perhaps he was the one who'd killed Mrs Solomon's cat.

'You wait – she'll be really pleased,' he said.

'What do I tell her?'

Buddy's heart skipped a beat – it was the first sign that she might do it.

'Just say we've found out that there's something going on in 56 and we've got proof, then ask her if she'll ring the cops.'

'Blimey, Buddy, I don't know. What do we tell them?'

'Just that you've seen someone break into the house, that's all. I'd do it myself but they might think I'm a kid playing a joke. Please, Char, please. Mrs Solomon's the only one who can do it. You don't have to give the number or anything. Just make sure they send someone round.'

Charmian walked away and stood at the edge of the shed, staring out at the rain. Suddenly she stepped out on to the wet playground.

Buddy ran after her, calling, 'Char!'

She stopped and turned round to him. Drops of rain were caught in the wiry tangle of her hair and the splashes on her face were making shiny lines on her skin. He felt that she was older and wiser than he was.

'OK,' she said. 'But I'm not doing it for Mrs Solomon or your dad, I'm doing it for you.'

'Thanks.'

Despite what she'd just said, he felt lonely and lost.

When he left her – she wanted to go to Croxley Street alone – he walked slowly through the rain. He felt the damp seep through on to his shoulders. Trickles ran down his neck and the rain soaked his shoes and the legs of his trousers. From out of nowhere he found himself hoping that he would catch pneumonia and die. He saw himself lying in a bed, surrounded by all the people he knew. They were crying and saying how sorry they were that they'd been horrible to him, but it was too late.

The following morning, Charmian was waiting for him outside the school gates.

'I saw Mrs Solomon – she said she'd do it.'

'Great – I told you she'd be pleased.'

'Maybe, but I'm still scared.'

There was nothing he could say, because he was scared, too.

## Chapter Eighteen

Lots of times in the next couple of days, Buddy felt like calling the whole thing off. He went over and over the plan until his head felt as if it was burning. He noticed that his hands had started to shake and he often found his foot tapping madly on its own.

'What's the matter wiv you? You're like a cat on 'ot bricks,' his dad said on Thursday evening.

Buddy said it was nothing and tried harder not to let his nervousness show. If his dad knew what he was planning, he'd go crazy. Supposing he found out afterwards?

This thought sent his brain spinning. Yet again, he went through the plan. Was there any way that someone could find out? Mrs Solomon would call the police to say that someone was breaking into 56. When they arrived and found Mr King with a lot of stolen things, he would think that it had all been caused by the nosiness of a neighbour. No one could possibly link it to Buddy. As for his dad, he would just think that it was a stroke of luck that Buddy had got his mum to come round at that particular time. No, it was perfect – he must stop worrying.

It was easier said than done, of course, and that night he lay awake for hours. The sky was growing light when finally he fell asleep and he couldn't have slept for more than a couple of hours before the alarm clock woke him. Yet, strangely, he felt great. All his doubts and fears of the night were gone. He was certain that he was doing the right thing and that it would all go well.

Just before he left for school, his dad came down and asked him to change his bandages again. The cuts were healing well and he could move all his fingers, but his face was still pale and worn from the pain and the worry. Well, after tonight, all the worrying would be over. Buddy wanted to say something, to tell him it would be all right, but he went on tying the bandages and lowered his head to hide the hope and pleasure that was making him smile madly.

During the day, he found himself ticking off the hours like the countdown to the launching of a spaceship. Seven fifteen was zero hour. At lunchtime, he saw Charmian and went over everything again. He said that seven thirty would be early enough for her to arrive at Mrs Solomon's but she said she'd be there at seven just to make sure. Then they went together to find Julius. Charmian had said that it would be better to tell him the truth but Buddy had refused, so they had to give him an alibi about where they were going to be.

'Jules,' Charmian said when they found him, 'we want you to keep a secret.'

'Yeah – what?'

'Promise you won't say?'

'OK. What is it?'

'I'm not going to the Satellite tonight but you mustn't tell Mum.'

'Where you going?'

'She's coming out with me,' Buddy said.

Julius burst out laughing. 'You dirty old man.'

Buddy blushed and he saw Charmian lower her eyes. Julius was going to tease them for ever about this, but it had to be done. Julius giggled and made all kinds of jokes but he agreed not to tell his parents that Charmian hadn't been at the club.

The afternoon lessons seemed endless but the hours at home were worse. Whenever he looked at his watch, he couldn't believe how slowly the minutes were passing. He stayed in his room because he didn't want his dad to see how tense he was but he felt like a wild animal trapped in a cage. He stared out of the window without really seeing anything until nearly six o'clock then went down to make the tea.

He was just cutting the bread for some sandwiches when a terrible thought struck him. The knife slipped and sliced into his finger next to the nail. There was a stab of pain but he took no notice of it. Mrs Solomon's phone number – he didn't know her phone number. He rushed out of the kitchen door and ran along the side path, ducking low so that his dad wouldn't see him through the window.

He'd planned everything so carefully. On Wednesday evening he'd even made the journey from his house to 56 Croxley Street in order to check how long it took. Yet now, at the last moment, there were still essential things that he hadn't done.

He ran down the road towards the telephone box, hoping desperately that her number would be in the directory. If it wasn't, what could he do? It would throw out all the timing if he couldn't ring Charmian there.

Someone was in the phone box. He stood outside and noticed the blood dripping from his finger. He sucked it, then pulled off the flap of loose skin. It wasn't a bad cut but the blood kept swelling out of it so he wrapped his paper handkerchief round it.

The man was still talking on the phone. Buddy looked at his watch – nearly six fifteen. Only an hour to go. Hurry up!

At last, the man put down the phone and pushed the door open. Buddy dived in and grabbed the directory. He flicked the pages. P, Q, R, S. Se, Sk, Sn, then finally So. Sollit, Solly and then, Solomon. He went down the list with his finger and there it was – Solomon Mrs L. E., 54 Croxley Street – 218179. He repeated the number until he was sure he knew it, then chanted it to himself all the way home.

He dashed upstairs, tore a bit of paper from the back of an exercise book and scribbled the number. It looked strange, written down. Had he got it right? Panic began to rise in him but he fought it down. Of course it was right. He sat on the bed, breathing deeply and pressing his finger until it hurt. Blood started to soak through the white paper and it throbbed horribly, but it stopped his crazy thoughts. He must stay calm.

'Buddy – I thought you was gonna make the tea,' his dad called from downstairs.

'Sorry, just coming.'

His finger made it awkward to cut the bread but he managed to make a couple of rather thick cheese sandwiches. He took them, with a cup of tea, into the front room and gave them to his dad.

'Where's yours?' his dad asked.

'I've eaten them,' Buddy lied – the very thought of food made him feel sick.

'Looks as if you've been eating your finger, too.'

'Oh, I just cut it. I'll go and put something on it,' Buddy said, glad of an excuse to get away.

He went to the bathroom, washed his finger and wrapped a plaster round it then sat on the edge of the bath gazing at the numbers ticking away on his watch. At exactly ten past seven he stood up and walked slowly and deliberately downstairs.

'I'm going down the Satellite,' he said, from the doorway of the front room.

'OK. See you later. I'll probably be back before you.'

Buddy nodded, opened the front door and left the house. This was it.

He waited at the end of the road. His face was hot and his heart was beating fast but he wouldn't let himself look at his watch. There was nothing to worry about. There was plenty of time and his mum had promised she wouldn't be late. Even so, he kept peering back in the direction of his house to make sure there was no sign of his dad leaving yet.

When a bus appeared in the distance, Buddy allowed himself a quick peek at the time – seven twenty-five. She had to be on this one – unless, of course, she'd decided to walk. The bus drew up at the stop. Somebody had got off but he couldn't see who because the bus was in the way. The driver accelerated and the bus pulled away. It was his mum. She was wearing a shiny black raincoat and her face looked white and serious. Halfway across the main road she saw him and nodded. A car was coming fast and she waited until it passed then strolled towards him with her hands in her pockets.

'Well, here I am,' she said. 'Don't ask me why.'

'You look nice.'

'I suppose that's something.'

Her voice was flat and she barely looked at him. They walked slowly along the pavement and he felt that she was hanging back, not wanting to get there. He stopped three houses away from his house.

'Aren't you coming?' she asked, surprised.

'I thought it would be better if you . . .' He couldn't finish the sentence and he looked at her helplessly.

'Great,' she said bitterly, then strode off towards the house. She rang the bell and Buddy pressed himself flat against the wall. When he peeped out, the door was open, casting a shaft of light on his mum, but he couldn't see his dad. His mum was talking. She smiled then stepped inside.

As soon as the door closed, Buddy ran past before they could get into the front room – his dad mustn't see him. He glanced quickly at the window but kept running.

She had been smiling when she went in – that must be a good sign. She'd just been nervous, that was why she'd snapped at him. It would be all right now.

He got to the telephone box. It was empty. He picked up the phone, checked the number on the piece of paper and dialled. Fancy panicking about Mrs Solomon's number – he could easily have looked it up now instead of earlier. That just showed how he worried unnecessarily. Everything was going perfectly. At this very minute, his mum and dad were together again after all this time – and he was the one who had done it.

The pips went and he put the coin in.

'Buddy?' Charmian's voice was breathless and excited.

'Yes. It's OK – my mum's there. I'm on my way.'

'He's here, Buddy. Mr King. He got here about quarter past seven. I watched him from the window. He's early.'

'That's all right.'

'Shall I get Mrs Solomon to ring now?'

Buddy looked at his watch. Seven forty-one. Why not? If he was there already, it didn't matter what time they rang. On the other hand it might be best to stick to the plan.

'No. Wait until eight.'

'Oh, Buddy, please. I want to get it over with.'

She sounded a bit panicky. If he ran most of the way, he could be there in about a quarter of an hour. How long would the police take once they got the phone call? Ten minutes? At least that. He could afford to let her ring a bit earlier.

'OK. You can ring at seven fifty – but not before. I'll be there as soon as I can.'

'Right.'

He slammed the phone down and started to run. The backstreets were deserted but each time he came to a main road there was still a lot of traffic and he had to wait before he could cross. The cold air hurt his lungs but he ran until his legs began to give out then slowed to a fast walk. He passed the cinema where he'd first told the twins about the house all those weeks ago and a couple of minutes later he was in Malham Road.

Seven fifty-three. Mrs Solomon must have rung by now. Perhaps the police were already on their way. The thought drove him on and he started running again. He could see the main road ahead. Over that, past the Germayne Arms, and he would be in Croxley Street. A few more minutes.

He reached the main road and stood panting, waiting for a gap in the traffic. He looked across to the Germayne Arms. A man emerged from the darkness of Croxley Street on to the brightly lit forecourt of the pub. There was a break in the traffic and Buddy was halfway across the road before he realized that the man was Mr King.

He stopped in horror and watched Mr King walk to the door and go into the pub. A car horn honked and Buddy ran the rest of the way to the pavement just in time. Someone yelled at him from the car but he didn't care.

He raced up to the pub door and pushed it open slightly. Mr King was standing at the bar talking to the barman. Buddy prayed that he was only buying something like cigarettes but his heart sank as he saw the barman draw a pint of beer and put it on the counter. Mr King paid, picked up the glass, and walked over to a table. He took off his overcoat and sat down. This was no quick drink – he was staying there.

Buddy let go of the door and dashed away down Croxley Street.

# Chapter Nineteen

What had gone wrong? Supposing the police came now –
the house would be empty. Had Charmian seen Mr King
leave? Would she ring the police again and say there'd
been a mistake?

His lungs were on fire and he could hear each rasping
breath he took. His head was pounding and the street
lights danced and jumped in front of him. A car drove
past. Was it the police? His eyes were full of tears and he
couldn't see properly. He brushed his hands across them
and blinked. Now the car was too far away to see but it
didn't seem to be slowing. No, it was disappearing into the
distance and he was nearly there.

He staggered past number 56 and pushed open the gate
to Mrs Solomon's house. He misjudged the first step up to
the front door and went sprawling, banging his knee. He
pulled himself to his feet and limped the rest of the way up
the flight of steps.

As he reached the porch, the front door opened and Charmian was there. In the hall, behind her, Buddy glimpsed Mrs Solomon sitting in her wheelchair. He opened his mouth to speak but nothing came out.

'He's gone,' Charmian shouted and her eyes were wide with worry. Mrs Solomon just put the phone down. I went into the room. She saw him. She rang when you said. What are we going to do?'

Buddy shook his head and felt his stomach heave. He leaned over the edge of the stairway but, although a bitter taste flooded the back of his throat, he couldn't be sick. He gulped hard and stood up.

'Ring,' he croaked. 'Got to ring them.'

'No, Buddy, we can't. Just let them come. Mrs Solomon didn't say who she was or anything. They won't know it was us.'

'He'll get away.'

'We can't help it. Come in and I'll get you a drink.'

Charmian headed for the kitchen and Buddy leaned against the door frame and slid down into a crouch, his face almost between his knees. When he raised his head again he saw Mrs Solomon. She hadn't moved. She looked at him then started stroking the cats on her lap and smiling as if the whole thing was a good joke.

Charmian came back with a glass of water. He took a couple of sips to clear his throat then drank half of it in one go. He felt it gurgle and slosh down to his stomach. Then he drank the rest, a gulp at a time, cooling the rawness of his throat.

'Come in and let me close the door,' Charmian said.

He shook his head. He didn't want to stay here in this mad woman's house. Far away, he heard a roar. The police, probably. He forced himself up and handed the glass to Charmian.

'I'm going,' he said.

The roar was getting louder. Charmian had noticed it now. She moved her head slightly to hear it better.

'It's them, they're coming,' she said, pulling at his arm and beginning to close the door.

Buddy shrugged himself free. If he was quick, he could be in the shadows on the other side of the road before they arrived. He heard Charmian shout as he dodged out of the closing door. At the bottom of the steps he stopped. The door had slammed behind him, but that wasn't what he was listening to. That roar didn't come from a car. It was a motorbike. Had they sent a motorbike cop?

He tore along the path to the garden gate. The bike was nearly there – no time to get across the road now. He saw the dazzling headlight, heard the engine rev as the driver changed down. The headlight beam swept in towards the pavement. The engine roared, then cut out as the bike glided to a stop. The light went out. Buddy peered round the gatepost.

It was his dad.

He was wearing his helmet but Buddy knew him by the bandages on his hands. He swung off the bike, rocked it back on to its stand and pulled his chinstrap. He took the helmet off and rested it on the seat, then began feeling his hands and flexing the fingers as if they were stiff and painful.

Buddy stepped out on to the pavement. His dad glanced up and, even in the dim light, the shock showed on his face.

'What the 'ell are you doing 'ere?'

'Why aren't you with Mum?' Buddy's voice was hoarse and he cleared his throat painfully.

'You 'ad no right to do that, Buddy.'

'What happened?'

'What d'you think 'appened?'

'Did she go?'

'Course she went. You 'ad no right.'

Buddy saw it all. Saw them standing awkwardly in the hall. They probably hadn't even got as far as the front room. It was his fault, but he hated them. Both of them. He might have guessed that his dad would freeze up and not say anything – he always did. And his mum, she could be so sarcastic when she wanted to. He remembered the way his heart had shrivelled when she'd said 'Great!' and just walked away. In a mood like that, she was bound to have said something horrible. And the row would have started. Just like before. Just like always. He hated them. They would never get back together.

'I told the police,' he said suddenly and then repeated it slowly, wanting every word to hurt his dad as much as possible.

His dad looked at him, puzzled, then his eyes grew wide as it sank in. He glanced over Buddy's shoulder, then he turned slowly and looked back along the road in the other direction.

'When?' he said. Buddy had expected anger, expected even to be hit, but the slow movements and the gentleness of his dad's voice threw him.

'Ten minutes ago.'

His dad turned back and looked directly at him.

'He made you do it,' Buddy said. 'I wanted the cops to get him so you could stop.'

His dad spun round and dashed towards the gate of 56. Buddy ran after him and grabbed his arm.

'He's not there. He's gone. I saw him go into the pub.'

'Des King?'

Buddy nodded.

'What about Ralph?'

Ralph? Was there someone else? Charmian hadn't said anything about anyone else. Then it hit him – Ralph James Campbell. The Beast. In Buddy's plan, the Beast had hardly counted as a real person at all. He hadn't actually wanted him to get into trouble, like Mr King, but he hadn't seemed important enough to worry about. One look at his dad's face changed that – to him, the Beast was a man called Ralph, a man who mattered.

'Was Ralph with Des?' his dad shouted and he grabbed hold of him and shook him. Buddy was glad. He wanted his dad to shake and shake him until he fell to pieces but his bandaged hands were still weak and they slipped off Buddy's arms.

'Was he?' his dad shouted.

'No.'

His dad ran towards the house then turned and yelled, 'Go. Now. Get away.'

When his dad disappeared down the side alley towards the back of the house, Buddy ran to the gateway of number 54. As he opened the gate, he caught a flash of blue light out of the corner of his eye. The light came again, sending a blue flicker across the branches of the trees. Then Buddy saw the car further down the road. It was moving slowly as if the occupants were checking the houses to find the right one. No siren – that would give the alarm.

The blue light flashed round and round, almost hypnotizing him until, at the last moment, he drew back behind the hedge. There was a soft scrunch from the tyres as the car came nearer. The light stabbed through the hedge and he crouched down and closed his eyes.

He stayed there, holding his breath and straining to hear something. Nothing. Total silence. Had it gone past? He opened his eyes. There was no blue light. Perhaps they had missed the house. There might be time to dash in and give the warning before they came back. He stood up, stepped out of the gate and froze.

The car was there, parked outside number 56. All its lights were off. They must be waiting before going in. Mad ideas filled his head. He could run past and pretend he was the one who'd broken into the house. Or he could go up to them and say that he'd seen some people run out of the house five minutes ago. Or he could pretend he was ill and had to go to hospital. Anything to give his dad time to get away.

He walked quickly to the car and bent down to open the door. It was empty.

He'd heard nothing. No engine noise. No opening and closing of doors. It was as if it was a ghost car. And as silently as ghosts, the police had left the car and gone into the house. It was too late; there was nothing he could do.

He ran to the other side of the road and hid himself in the deep shadows under a low-hanging tree. The blood was pulsing round his body, filling his ears with its throb. Two cars passed, the drivers automatically slowing to look at the police car. Time ticked by with the beating of his blood and he began to count. One, two . . .

When he reached 135, he saw Mr King walking through the pool of light under a lamp post a long way down the road. He watched him walk steadily out of the light into darkness and then into the light of a nearer lamp post. He was whistling. When he saw the police car, he stopped as suddenly as if he had walked into an invisible wall. He stood still for a moment then took a couple of steps backwards before turning and walking quickly away. Buddy watched him until he disappeared in the far darkness.

He started to count again. He reached 500 and went back to the beginning. It was taking a long time. Perhaps his dad had got out in time and run away across the back gardens. Perhaps he was still in the house, talking to the police, convincing them that he had every right to be there, that the phone call had been a false alarm. The thoughts muddled up his counting. Better not to think, better just to count his heartbeats. He started again.

He reached 500 twice more and then had to stop because the pounding of his blood had faded until he could no longer count his heartbeats. He looked at his watch – eight thirty-five. How long had they been inside? The front door of number 54 opened and Charmian was framed in the light from the hall. She made large beckoning signs to him with her arm. Could she see him here in the shadows, or had she been watching every movement since the whole thing began? He didn't move. She started to signal again then looked sideways at number 56 and ducked back inside the door.

A moment later a policeman stepped out from the gateway. He was carrying the briefcase that had the jewellery in it. He got into the front of the car, leaving the door open. Buddy saw him speak and heard the tinny reply of the radio. Then his dad came out of the gate, followed by the Beast and another policeman. His dad went straight to the car, opened the back door and got in. He slid along the seat to allow the Beast in. The policeman closed the door behind them, then walked round the car and got into the front seat.

The driver was still talking into the microphone and his door was open, so the inside light was on. Buddy could see his dad clearly. He lay back against the seat and closed his eyes. Then the Beast leaned forward and put his head in his hands as if he were crying. His dad sat up and put his arm round the Beast's shoulder.

The front door slammed. The light went off. The engine purred into life, and, as silently as it had arrived, the car drew away.

The whole thing had been so calm. His dad and the Beast hadn't been held or pushed. They'd got into the car as if it had been a taxi. The policeman had closed the door politely behind them. It had looked as if they had been going to a funeral. That was why the Beast had cried. Someone must be dead.

His dad's bike was still there.

Buddy walked across and pulled it off its stand. He couldn't push it all the way home. He'd have to leave it somewhere safe. He bumped it up on to the pavement, wheeled it into Mrs Solomon's garden and parked it on her lawn. He took out the keys and slipped them into his pocket. His dad could . . . could . . . pick it up when he came back from the funeral.

Buddy stayed by the bike, staring at it. There was nowhere to go. Mrs Solomon's front door closed and he heard footsteps.

Charmian took hold of his arm. 'You'd better come with me, Buddy.' She pulled and he let himself be led away.

# *Chapter Twenty*

Buddy sat on the sofa at the Rybeeros while Charmian told her mum what had happened. He didn't really listen properly but he heard her mention his dad, his mum, the plan, the police. Once or twice, she got bits wrong but he didn't bother to correct her. He didn't even care when Julius came back and the whole story was told again. It didn't matter any more. Soon everybody would know. It would be in the local paper next week, perhaps it would even be in the daily paper tomorrow. The people in 3E would know. Mr Normington would know. He didn't care.

He didn't say a word.

Mrs Rybeero gave him a drink and made up the spare bed in Julius's room. She left the room while he took off his clothes and got into bed, then she came back in and talked gently to him. He noticed odd details about her face – the chubby black cheeks, her brown eyes – but he barely heard a word she said. She turned off the light and went away.

He closed his eyes but he didn't sleep. He saw his dad putting his arm round the Beast's shoulders. They hadn't been going to a funeral; they'd been going to the police station. Were they there now, or were they already in prison? How did the police make their cars go so silently?

He heard Julius come in and get into bed. There was a whisper from the other side of the room. 'Buddy, you asleep?'

He didn't reply.

When he woke next morning, it took him a moment to remember where he was and what had happened. Julius's bed was empty. He turned over and went back to sleep.

He pulled out of a strange dream to find Mrs Rybeero shaking his shoulder. 'Hello, Buddy, you want some food?'

'I don't want breakfast,' he mumbled and was aware of the thickness in his throat.

'Breakfast! Dear child, you already sleep through breakfast, lunch and supper. Here, drink something. Soup – it give you belly something to work on.'

He sat up and she handed him a mug of soup. The bedroom light was on and the window showed the darkness outside. It was five past eight according to his watch. Twenty-four hours ago, he'd been in Croxley Street. Twenty-four hours ago, he could have stopped it all.

'Come on now, you drink the soup,' Mrs Rybeero said, sitting on the edge of the bed. 'You been out of it a long time and you still out of it, seem to me.'

He sipped the soup. It tasted good and it wasn't too hot so he gulped it until it was all gone. He gave the mug back to Mrs Rybeero and lay down. He felt weak and tired even though he'd slept for nearly a whole day.

'Buddy, what you mother telephone number? Ah better ring her and tell her you here.'

'It's all right – I'll go round and see her tomorrow.' It was a lie and he suddenly knew what he was really going to do.

'You do that, Buddy – best to let her know. But if you want, you can stay here as long as you like.'

Buddy nodded and she left, turning out the light. It was kind of her to say he could stay but that wouldn't do any good. He was on his own. His dad would go to prison, perhaps for years, and his mum wouldn't want him after all this. As soon as the police found out that he didn't have anyone to look after him, he'd have to go into 'a Home' of some sort. 'In care' they called it. He'd be in some house with lots of others, like a big, lonely factory where the last thing anybody did was care. That was what always happened. Well, they wouldn't do it to him. First thing in the morning, he'd get out of here before they found him.

In fact, it was late again when he woke – nearly eleven thirty in the morning. He got dressed quickly and was surprised how weak he felt. His legs were wobbly and his head started to spin when he went to the bathroom. He would have liked to go back to bed but he bent over the washbasin and splashed water on his face to wake himself up.

Mrs Rybeero was in the kitchen when he went downstairs. She made him sit at the table and eat some cereal and toast.

'The twins at church with me husband. Ah stay here less you wake up and wonder where we go to.'

Buddy ate quickly because he wanted to get away as soon as possible. Mrs Rybeero tried to make him stay for Sunday dinner but he told her that he wanted to see his mum before she started worrying.

'Sure, ah understand,' Mrs Rybeero said as she led the way through into the office and unlocked the front door. Then she put both hands on his shoulders and looked him in the eyes.

'Ah know what you feeling, Buddy – but don't you go blaming you daddy, now. It easy to do wrong – we all do it some time or other. That why Jesus say, "He who without sin, let him cast the first stone." Remember that, now.'

He nodded quickly and slipped out of the door before she started on again.

Everything seemed slightly strange, as if he were back in the world after a long, long absence. The sky was covered with an unbroken white cloud but the light dazzled him more than if the sun had been shining brightly. The shops were closed and the streets were grimy and ugly. The few people he met hardly looked at him and he felt remote from them as if they weren't real human beings at all.

At the end of his road, he waited for a bit to check whether there was anybody hanging around near his house. All the cars were the usual ones, but he went past his house on the opposite pavement to make sure there was nobody hiding somewhere else. It appeared safe enough. He doubled back quickly, key at the ready, and opened the front door.

He listened. No sound. The house smelled stale and unlived-in already. He went up to his bedroom and tipped his school things out of the red canvas bag. It wouldn't hold very much but he couldn't wander around with a big suitcase. He pulled open a drawer and began selecting things to take. A couple of shirts, socks, underwear and three thick sweaters. He crammed them into the bag but they wouldn't all fit. He'd wear one of the sweaters and leave one behind. He went to the bathroom and emptied the big plastic laundry bag on the floor. He grabbed a towel, some soap, toothpaste and his toothbrush and went back to his room.

Buddy rolled up his sleeping bag as small as he could and stuffed it into the plastic bag with the toilet things. He ran downstairs, got a knife and went out into the back garden. The knife was blunt and he had to saw at the rope of the washing line but finally he cut a bit of the right length. At the same time he realized that he'd need a knife, fork and spoon and he picked them up when he went back inside. A can opener, too – that would be useful.

He forced the cutlery down the side of his canvas bag then set to work rolling up the plastic bag. It took ages until he got it right but he was pleased with the result. It was shaped like a sausage and tied at both ends with the rope. When he slipped the rope over his head and under one arm, it sat snugly on his back. He slung the canvas bag over his shoulder, took a last look at his room, then went to his dad's room.

Buddy knew his dad always kept some money in the top drawer of the bedside cabinet but he was surprised how much there was – eighty-three pounds. With that, and the eleven pounds of his own, he had enough to last for weeks. He stuffed it into his back pocket and went downstairs. He opened the front door slightly to check that the police hadn't arrived while he'd been busy, then ran out and down the road.

# Chapter Twenty-one

There was an anxious moment when he got to the bus station. Just as he started to cross the road, a patrol car drew up outside. He turned back and pretended to look in a shop window. Reflected in the glass, he saw a policeman get out and go into the bus station. Surely they wouldn't be looking for him here. It wasn't as if he were a criminal. Then Buddy saw the policeman take out some coins and put them in the cigarette machine. He got his packet, walked to the car and drove off.

Buddy spent the next half hour working out where to go. He studied the big map and chose two possible places in the Forest area, but when he checked the timetables he found that there were no Sunday buses to either of them.

In the end, he had to settle for a bus going to West Axle. It was in the exact opposite direction from the Forest but there were large green areas marked on the map. It didn't really matter where it was, as long as it was away from the city. If he could only find some old barn, he'd stay there until he'd decided what to do.

The bus didn't leave until three twenty so he had over an hour to kill. He went into the snack bar and bought two rolls, some chocolate and a cup of tea then deliberately sat at the corner table where he'd sat with his mum. He nibbled at a roll but he didn't feel very hungry. In fact, he didn't feel anything except flat and drained. It was as though, since his long sleep, he was empty of emotion. He was doing important and unusual things but it was all happening at a distance from him and none of it really touched him.

He looked at the chair where his mum had sat. It had all just been talk that night. She'd said a lot but when it had come to doing something, really trying to talk to his dad and make it work, she'd hardly done a thing.

At exactly three twenty the bus pulled out of the garage and drew up at the stop. Buddy grabbed his things and followed a couple of other people out of the snack bar and on to the bus. He went upstairs and sat at the front.

The journey was terribly long and he stared out of the window at the dull houses and gardens. There were few people around and the world seemed grey, half dead and a long way away. By the time they were out in the open countryside, it was beginning to grow dark. The sun had gone down behind huge black clouds that were moving in from the south-west. He wouldn't have much time to find somewhere to spend the night and it looked as if it might rain.

At last the bus came to a crossroads and he saw a sign that said 'West Axle 4 miles'. To his surprise, the bus turned left off the main road in another direction. He clattered down the stairs and asked the conductor why.

'This is the route,' the man said. 'We go via Ramsett and Dryford first. We don't get to West Axle for another forty-five minutes.'

Forty-five minutes – it would be dark by then. He looked at the passing countryside. Here would be as good a place as any.

'Can you let me off at the next stop, please?'

A couple of minutes later, Buddy was standing at the roadside watching the bus disappearing down the lane. Apart from the small wooden bus shelter, there was nothing but open fields and a clump of trees off to the right. The loneliness frightened him. Back in the city it had seemed a good idea to get away from the street lights and the houses and the traffic, but this silent, still landscape was terrifying. Much better to be near people. Surely there must be a farm round here where he could hide in a barn and yet know that there was somebody nearby.

He started walking in the direction that the bus had gone. The light was fading fast and there were a few drops of rain on the wind. He began to jog. The rope holding the plastic bag on his back was too tight and it cut into his chest but there was no time to stop and loosen it. The canvas bag kept slipping off his shoulder so he took it off and ran with it in his arms. There was a bend in the road ahead and he sprinted towards it, hoping that there would be some sign of life. There wasn't. As far as he could see, the road stretched away into empty darkness.

Sheer desperation kept him going. The conductor had mentioned the names of two villages – they had to be somewhere along the road. When he finally saw a glimmer of light far away on his right, his heart leaped. Yet the road seemed to be taking him away from it. Should he try and make his way towards it across the fields? He'd almost made up his mind to do that, when he saw an opening in the hedge and a track leading off in the direction of the light.

The track was muddy and pitted with deep holes and ruts but he groped along it, seeing the light grow nearer and nearer. There was a pattering on the ground and the rain began to beat down. He'd found this place just in time – a few more minutes and he would be sheltering in one of the buildings that were beginning to loom out of the darkness. Then, ahead of him, he heard a growl. He stopped.

The growl came again, then a dog started barking wildly. Another dog joined in, further away at first, but coming closer. In the dimness, he saw two large shapes standing in the middle of the track. They were edging slowly towards him, barking and growling fiercely.

A door opened in the house and a man's voice called out something. Buddy turned and ran. The rain blew into his face and he slipped and stumbled on the uneven ground but the thought of the dogs kept him running until he reached the road. Even then, he walked fast. He couldn't go on like this – fumbling around trying to find a farm. There was only one thing to do – take the long road back to where he'd got off the bus. At least it would be dry in the bus shelter and there wasn't much chance that anybody else would use it tonight.

By the time he got there, he was soaked. He dumped his bags in a corner and stood shivering against the back wall. It was pitch black outside and the only sound was the rain beating on the roof. The shivering grew worse and he knew he ought to get out of his wet clothes. There was nowhere else to go so he might as well resign himself to spending the night here.

He undid the plastic bag and laid the sleeping bag on top of it. His clothes clung to him but he pulled them off and slipped into his sleeping bag, wearing only his T-shirt and underpants. He was so cold that he didn't care how ridiculous the whole thing was. Bit by bit, he warmed up and the shivering stopped.

Two cars passed during the course of the long evening. Each time, the headlights dazzled him and he felt sure that he would be seen but the cars swept past without even slowing down. The rest of the time he lay in total darkness with his head pillowed on the canvas bag. He ate a piece of chocolate but although he knew he needed it for warmth, he could barely swallow it. Once or twice he dozed off but the cold and the hardness of the ground woke him up again.

For long periods of time, he lost all sense of where he was. His body grew numb and his eyes stared into complete blackness. Only the sound of the rain told him that the world still existed.

He jerked out of sleep straight up into a sitting position. Small, cold feet had just run across his face. He felt something fall on to his sleeping bag and scuttle away. Although it had probably only been a mouse, the shock broke his nerve. There could be anything here, in the dark – rats, weasels, stoats. A fox could be baring its teeth at him only a few feet away from his face and he wouldn't see it. He hunched himself down in the sleeping bag and pulled the ends over his head. The movement made him aware of how cold he was and the uncontrollable shivering began again.

He slept fitfully, coming up for air every so often then sliding back down into the bag. Gradually, the rain eased and finally stopped though water continued to drip from the shelter for a long time afterwards. When, at last, he saw the sky start to grow lighter, he relaxed.

A roar woke him up and he opened his eyes in time to see the huge wheels of a tractor roll by only a few feet away from the entrance to the shelter. He sat up painfully as the roar faded away. A grey mist hid the far side of the road and the air was chilly and damp but it was daytime. Five minutes later he was dressed and ready to go. He'd put on a dry shirt and sweater but his jeans were still sopping wet and they clung to his legs clammily. Even the money in his back pocket was damp. His shoes, too, were wet and were already soaking through the dry socks he'd put on. He stuffed the sleeping bag back into the plastic bag, not bothering to roll it properly or tie it with the rope. Picking it up, he slung the canvas bag over his shoulder and walked stiffly out of the bus shelter, leaving his wet clothes piled in a corner.

He headed towards the main road, feeling his numbed body begin to come back to life. The idea of living rough in the country had been mad, he saw that now. Much better to be in the city he'd known all his life. There were plenty of places he could hide and one, in particular, where nobody would think of looking for him.

As he stood at the crossroads waiting for a lift into town, he realized what day it was: Monday. It was his birthday. He was fourteen.

# Chapter Twenty-two

Yesterday he'd done everything in such a rush and had made many bad decisions but this time he planned more carefully. He went to a supermarket and chose food that would keep a long time and also got essential things like matches, candles and lavatory paper. At another shop he bought a little camping stove, a spare canister of gas and a small saucepan. Lastly, he bought some adhesive tape in case he needed to break a window to get into the house.

He was a bit worried that someone might see him in town but the only really dangerous moment came when he got near the house. If Mrs Solomon happened to spot him out of the window, there was always the chance that she might say something to somebody. It was a risk he had to take, though. He ran down the alleyway at the side of number 56, keeping as close to the wall as possible. He rounded the corner and then peeped up at Mrs Solomon's side window. It was empty and he felt sure that he hadn't been seen.

As he'd expected, the back door of 56 was locked and the little larder window was closed. The police would have come back after Friday evening to check if there were any more stolen goods in the house and they would have made sure everything was closed up after they left.

He found some loose bricks in the garden and piled them up high enough for him to reach the window. Tearing strips of adhesive tape, he covered the whole pane of glass with it. Then he got a stone and smashed it hard against the window. The glass shattered but made hardly any noise. He peeled the tape off carefully, bringing most of the glass with it, and reached inside to unlatch the window. He pulled it open and began trying to climb up. It took all his strength but finally he heaved himself up and into the larder.

By the time he'd cleared up outside and brought all his things in, he felt exhausted. His jeans were still damp so he took them off and hung them in a corner then got into the sleeping bag and lay down on the camp bed.

It was strange to be lying on the Beast's bed. He pulled off his sweater and arranged it so that his head wouldn't be touching the canvas. The Beast wasn't dirty, but he was strange and perhaps you could catch the strangeness like a disease. He didn't want to end up like the Beast. Yet here he was, living in the Beast's room, sleeping in his bed.

He tried to tell himself that it wouldn't be for long but it didn't help. He'd hoped that he would feel more cheerful once he'd found somewhere safe to stay but, although he was better off here than in the bus shelter, he still felt depressed and lifeless. How long could he go on living like this? Sooner or later somebody would find him, wherever he was. Then they would put him in a Home. They'd probably still let him go to school, but that would be even worse. He could just imagine what some of the kids there would say and do. He'd try anything rather than have to face that. Yet each time it came back to that same problem – what could he do and where could he go? The questions went round and round in his head until he fell asleep.

It was totally dark when he woke and he thought he was back in the bus shelter. Then he realized that there was no sound of rain and he remembered where he was. The darkness frightened him and he groped across the room until he found the matches. The light from one candle wasn't enough to drive the shadows from the corners so he lit another two. His watch said one twenty and he assumed it must be early Tuesday morning. Since Friday, though, he'd spent so much time sleeping or half asleep that it wouldn't have surprised him if he'd slept through a whole day. Perhaps it was now Wednesday. Time didn't matter any more. He had nothing to do and nowhere to go.

Regular mealtimes didn't matter either so he decided to eat now. He lit the stove and heated up a tin of stew. He sat on the edge of the bed and started to eat it out of the saucepan. He wasn't as bad as the Beast yet – he ate his food cold, straight out of the tin. Charmian had noticed that the first time they'd come here. Charmian and Julius – what would they be doing now? Asleep, of course. They were leading proper lives, not eating meals in the middle of the night. And what about the Beast? In prison somewhere – all because of what Buddy had done. Not just the Beast, either. His dad.

Since Friday evening, Buddy hadn't allowed himself to think about his dad for more than a few seconds at a time. Now, however, there was no holding it back. He'd tried to forget it but every single moment of the evening was burned into his brain. The look his dad had given him when he'd said that he'd called the police. The calm way he'd got into the police car. The way he'd put his arm round the Beast's shoulder.

Buddy got up and put the saucepan in the old stone sink. He'd only eaten a couple of mouthfuls but he wasn't hungry any more. Until now, all he'd done was feel sorry for himself and worry about what was going to happen to him. But what about his dad? Being in prison was worse than being in a Home – they wouldn't have bars and locked doors in a Home. A terrible picture flashed across his mind – his dad alone in a cell, looking at the sky through a barred window.

He put out the candles and threw himself on the bed. All he wanted to do was sleep. Sleep and forget. That must be why people killed themselves – to forget. It was obvious, of course, but he'd never seen it so clearly before. The man who had owned this house, for instance. After he'd killed his wife, all he'd wanted to do was forget, but sleep hadn't been enough for him – he'd hanged himself to make sure that he never woke up and remembered.

Buddy was frightened in the dark but he wouldn't let himself light a candle. Being frightened stopped him thinking about other things. The house was full of sounds – creaks, rustlings and tappings. He lay, tense and motionless, listening to each one until gradually he came to know them all. They still scared him when they came suddenly after a long period of silence, but they were just noises. They would still be happening if he wasn't there to hear them. The noises didn't know he was there. The room didn't know he was there. The bed he was lying on didn't know he was lying on it. In fact, he wasn't even sure that he was lying on it. His body was lying on the bed, but suddenly he knew that his body wasn't him. People looked at his body and said, 'There's Buddy Clark,' but, in fact, his body was really only like a painting he'd seen in a film once. The painting was of a man's face and there were little flaps for the eyes. Somebody behind the painting had kept opening the eye flaps and looking out. Just like the real Buddy Clark now, tiny and hidden somewhere deep inside his body, was peering out through the holes in his head that people called eyes.

Shafts of light came in through the planks of wood nailed over the window. He watched them move slowly across the walls and ceiling as the day passed and night filled the room again.

Now there was a noise he hadn't heard before – a click, a scrape and a bang. Then footsteps. He froze in alarm and held his breath. The door opened and a huge shape, darker than the darkness, came into the room. A match flared. The figure bent down and lit a candle, then stood up. It was the Beast.

Buddy sat up and the Beast turned at the noise. His face was blank – no fear, not even surprise. He held the candle up higher so that the light fell more fully on Buddy. Then he seemed to remember something. He looked round the room.

'Where are the black boys?' he asked.

Buddy realized what he was talking about. 'They're not here. I'm by myself. One of them was a girl.'

The Beast nodded. He stared at Buddy for a long time, then shrugged his shoulders and busied himself lighting another two candles and putting them in the corners of the room, as though there was nothing more to be said. Buddy got off the bed and crossed quickly to get his jeans. The Beast saw what he was doing and turned his back while Buddy put them on.

'I'm sorry I'm in your house – I haven't got anywhere else to go,' he said, feeling that he owed the Beast some kind of explanation even though he didn't seem at all angry.

'It's my house,' the Beast said. 'Uncle Des told me, "It's your house, Ralphie, and that's that."'

Uncle Des. Des King. Was Mr King the Beast's uncle? The shock of seeing the Beast had driven all other thoughts out of his mind, but suddenly they all came rushing back. The Beast was out of prison. What had happened? Was his dad free, too?

'I thought you weren't here. I thought you were in prison. You went away with the police.'

The Beast's face looked just as it had done when Charmian had accused him of killing the cat.

'I didn't do anything. I didn't know,' he said, his voice full of a desperate desire to be believed. 'Mr Clark told them. He told them I didn't steal anything. Mr Clark told them.'

Of course he did, Buddy thought. His dad had put his arm round the Beast's shoulder. His dad would never have let the police accuse this simple man. He had undone some of the harm that Buddy had done. He had taken all the blame himself and the police had let the Beast go.

'I didn't steal anything,' the Beast repeated.

'I know. I know you didn't.'

The Beast looked relieved. A shy smile crept round his mouth. He folded his arms self-consciously then unfolded them and let them hang by his side. Buddy didn't know what to do. Should he go? The Beast didn't appear to be at all bothered about finding someone in his room. On the contrary, he seemed pleased.

'I brought a stove,' Buddy said, for something to say. 'You can cook your food on it.'

The Beast smiled and nodded, then looked hopefully at him. Buddy set to work. He took the saucepan outside and threw the remains of the stew into the garden, then went back and washed it. The Beast sat on the bed watching his every move. Buddy lit the stove and held up a selection of cans.

'You choose,' he said, but the Beast shook his head and pointed at Buddy. 'All right, then – beans.'

He opened two cans, poured them into the saucepan and put it on the stove. When the beans were hot enough, he put half of them back in the can and gave it to the Beast, who sat waiting with his fork poised until Buddy was ready to start. They each took a mouthful then nodded and smiled at each other to show they liked it. They ate slowly – Buddy, because he was really enjoying the taste of food after such a long time without eating properly, and the Beast, as though he had been taught that he must chew everything thoroughly before swallowing.

They didn't speak. Normally, Buddy would have been embarrassed at being in a room with someone without talking, but with the Beast it didn't seem to matter. They finished their food and while Buddy washed the saucepan and the cutlery, the Beast tidied things up. He stacked the unopened cans along one wall and took the others outside. Then he carefully lifted Buddy's things and piled them neatly against the other wall. Finally, he took the sleeping bag off the bed and put it in the middle of the floor. He arranged the blankets on the camp bed and lay down.

Buddy stood, unsure what to do. Well then, ask.

'Would you mind if I stayed?'

The Beast thought for a moment, and it was obvious that he was thinking – no attempt to cover up or pretend to be polite like most people. Finally he folded his arms across his chest and said, 'You can stay.'

Buddy lay on the sleeping bag. The yellow light from the candles flickered on the ceiling. He felt strangely peaceful and happy. It was good to be with another human being. As soon as he thought it, though, he felt a stab of sorrow. It couldn't last. He couldn't stay here. The Beast wouldn't want him here all the time. Besides, there was always the chance that Uncle Des would come.

He turned on to his side and looked over at the Beast. 'Is Uncle Des's name Mr King?' he asked, aware now of how easy it was to talk directly and simply to someone who was direct and simple.

The Beast rolled over and looked at him. 'Mr King,' he said, as if he was pleased that Buddy knew him. 'He's a good man. He said I didn't have to stay in Chandos House. I didn't like it there.'

Even if Buddy hadn't known what it was, there would have been no need to ask about Chandos House. The look on the Beast's face told everything. Chandos House was a mental home on the outskirts of the city, not far from Buddy's school. Kids at school often made jokes about it.

Buddy stared at the ceiling again. So, even Mr King wasn't as bad as he'd seemed. True, he'd used his simple nephew's house as a place for storing stolen goods, but at least he'd rescued him from a loony bin. And he certainly hadn't been responsible for getting him arrested – nobody but Buddy could claim that honour.

The candles began to burn low and the long shadows danced nearer and nearer each other. Buddy suddenly felt that he didn't want the darkness to come again. He wanted the warm light to last until he decided to put it out because he wanted to sleep – and perhaps not even then. It would be good to wake up and be able to see where he was.

As if he had read Buddy's thoughts, the Beast got up and lit three new candles from the stubs of the old ones. He brought one and put it near Buddy, then stood the other two near his own bed. He lay down again then raised himself on one elbow, staring at Buddy openly and without embarrassment. He looked as if he were about to say something but then just pointed at the candles and laughed gently. Buddy knew exactly what he meant – yes, it was silly to need the light to chase the dark away but it was good to have it.

'Haven't you got a mum and dad?' The Beast asked the question just like a little boy but there was something dangerous about it.

Buddy felt a slight sweat break out on his face. He shook his head. No mum and dad – that was what it felt like. They would certainly have stopped thinking of him as their son since Friday.

The Beast swung his legs round and sat on the edge of the bed. The news had really interested him. The candlelight shone in his dark eyes just as it had the night Buddy had seen him through the letterbox.

'I haven't got a mum and dad,' he said, staring intently at Buddy as if that made them brothers.

Buddy didn't know what to say.

The Beast's eyes wandered away towards the corner of the room but he wasn't seeing anything. He shook his head and spoke slowly and sadly. 'I haven't got . . .'

Buddy couldn't tell whether the Beast had forgotten the words or whether he just couldn't bear to say them again. The room had grown hot and stuffy in the last few minutes.

'You've got an uncle, though,' Buddy said, trying to break the tension.

The Beast nodded. Buddy thought rapidly – he felt uncomfortable in the silence – he wanted to keep talking to cover it up. Uncle – that was the brother of one of your parents.

'Was your Uncle Des, your dad's brother or your mum's brother?'

'My mum. Uncle Des was my mum's brother. My mum. My mum. My mum.'

The Beast's eyelids flicked wider. Buddy's ears popped as the pressure in the room seemed to change. He heard each whispered word and saw every movement that the Beast's mouth made in order to say, 'My – dad – killed – her.'

A shiver shot up Buddy's back like a shock wave. The news scrambled wildly round his brain and then suddenly lurched into position. The Beast was *their* son.

The Beast's eyes were totally blank. The pupils were huge. Buddy hardly dared imagine what those eyes were seeing from all those years ago. The young Ralph James Campbell – perhaps younger than Buddy – coming home from school and finding his mother on the floor surrounded by the blood that had poured from her throat. The young Ralph James Campbell calling for his father, running all over the house looking for him and finally finding him, hanging from a rope.

The eyes were blank and Buddy couldn't tear his gaze from them. They were empty like the eyes of the painting in that film. Perhaps, somewhere deep behind them, the real Ralph James Campbell was peering out of the holes at him – tiny and terrified.

The Beast's eyelids flickered and closed for a couple of seconds. When he opened them he was seeing things again. He smiled slightly at Buddy and then looked at the candles. Buddy's mind was still racing to cope with his shock and confusion and he leaped at the chance to say something, anything.

'I'm not tired. I'll keep the candles alight if you want to sleep.'

The Beast nodded and lay down on the bed. He covered himself with the blankets. A few minutes later, his whole body jerked slightly. He sighed deeply and Buddy knew he was asleep.

Buddy blew out two of the candles and put the other one directly in line with the Beast's face so that it would be the first thing he saw if he woke up. Then he sat on the floor at the far side of the room, staring at the candle's steady flame and waiting for his brain to calm down so that he could think. When the first candle was just a small flickering stump, he replaced it with a new one, then another. By the time the third candle had burned out, daylight was coming through the cracks in the window.

It hadn't been much – seeing the Beast through one night. Not much at all, after the trouble he had caused him by calling the police. But what could he do for him, anyway? There was only one thing that the Beast wanted, and nobody on earth could help him with that. His parents were dead and there was the end of it. But Buddy's weren't and no matter how difficult the situation was, it could never be as hopeless as the Beast's.

'Ralph,' he said, gently shaking his shoulder. The Beast's eyes opened sleepily but closed again. 'Can you hear me?' The Beast nodded. 'It's morning. I've got to go now. I'll see you around. OK? Thanks for letting me stay. Bye.'

'Bye,' he mumbled and snuggled down in sleep.

Buddy got his things together – leaving the food and the stove – and crept quietly out of the dark house.

## Chapter Twenty-three

It was cold out and there'd been a frost. Buddy was glad he hadn't spent last night in the open countryside. Nearly eight o'clock. If he hurried, he would catch his mum before she went to work. And then what? Tell her what had happened? Ask her to let him stay? He wouldn't try and plan what to say. He'd wait until he was there and then just talk simply and directly, the way he'd spoken to the Beast.

The cold air numbed his face and hands but the fast walking warmed his body. He tried what he thought might be a short cut but it got him lost in streets he didn't recognize so he had to double back until he knew where he was. He started running then; he didn't want to miss her.

It was just past eight thirty when he finally turned into Raynall Avenue. He sprinted along, checking the numbers, and arrived panting at the bottom of the basement steps of 23b. He rang the bell. Nobody was coming. Had she left already? He rang again and put his eye to the bobbly glass. The bobbles distorted everything but he saw a movement of light as the kitchen door opened. There was the sound of loud music and someone was coming down the hall.

He stepped back as the door opened. It was his mum's friend, Joyce. She was in her dressing gown and she looked as if she hadn't been up long.

'Is my mum in?'

'Buddy,' she said, her eyes opening wide and losing their sleepy look. 'Where've you been? Everybody's been looking for you. Are you all right?' She took hold of his arm and pulled him inside before he had a chance to speak.

He followed her along the corridor and into the kitchen. Music was blaring out from under a newspaper on the table. Joyce snatched the paper away and turned the radio off. She seemed almost angry and Buddy shuffled uncomfortably in the sudden silence. His eyes fixed on the newspaper – it was the midweek edition of the local paper.

'Where's my mum?'

Joyce didn't reply. Instead, she held out the newspaper. The blood drained from his face. Something terrible had happened. He grabbed the paper and his eyes flew across the page. He'd expected something about his mum but he found a photo of himself. It had been taken at school in the first year when his hair had been long. It didn't look anything like him now. Next to the photo were the words 'CITY BOY MISSING'. He read the first line then skipped down the short column – 'Friday night . . . staying with friends . . . Sunday . . . hunt . . . police . . . inquiries.'

He threw the paper down on the table. 'Where is she?'

'Round at your house. She's been going crazy with worry thanks to you. They both have.'

They? What did she mean? He could hardly get the words out. 'My dad's there?'

'Yes.'

'How?'

'He's out on bail. Your mum put up the bail.'

Joyce shouted something as he ran down the corridor but he didn't listen. He dropped his bags in his hurry to get out of the door and he didn't bother to pick them up.

When he got to the High Street, the pavements were filled with people and he had to dodge and twist round them. Some people stopped and glared at him as he rushed towards them and he wondered if any of them recognized him from the paper. His enemies in 3E had probably seen it, and he could just imagine what Mr Normington was thinking. But none of that mattered now. He could face whatever they said. All he wanted to do was get home.

A flicker of doubt crossed his mind as he slipped the key into the front door latch and he hesitated before turning it.

Then the door swung open and his mum was there, her face alight with relief. She threw her arms around him and, over her shoulder, Buddy saw his dad come out of the front room. His mum let go of him and he stepped inside, still looking at his dad.

His dad put his hands in his pockets and ducked his head in the direction of the door. 'Listen to me, Buddy Clark. You do two fings – cry, or say you're sorry and you're out that door. Right?'

Buddy gulped and shook his head.

'I didn't 'ear you say "yes".'

'Yes.'

'Right. And there's one other fing before your mum starts yakkin' on about where you been. Might be six or nine months before me trial comes up in court and I've promised your mum I'll get a job. You said them black friends of yours needed drivers . . .'

# Chapter Twenty-four

The night before the trial, his dad worked late. Buddy finished his homework and then helped his mum revise for her Business Studies exam the following week. He went through her notes and tested her on questions about accountancy and computers. Normally, she got them all right, but this evening she kept making silly mistakes. At eleven o'clock, she told him to go to bed and although he wanted to stay up, he didn't argue.

He couldn't sleep, though. He kept listening for the sound of his dad's taxi drawing up outside. Then he realized his dad wouldn't be bringing it home tonight because he wouldn't be driving tomorrow.

Well after midnight, he heard the front door open and close. There was the murmur of voices for a while then his mum came upstairs. He saw her pass his door and go into their bedroom. A couple of minutes later, his dad came up.

'Buddy – you asleep?'

'No.'

His dad came in and pushed the door to behind him. The door closed and then slipped open slightly as the catch failed to hold. His dad stood awkwardly for a moment then sat on the far end of the bed. A beam of light from the hall squeezed in past the edge of the door and caught his knees and his clasped hands, but his face was in shadow.

'I'm gonna plead guilty,' he said.

Buddy's heart started thumping.

'Might get a bit less like that – you never know your luck. Maybe a year, maybe less. Old Man Rybeero said 'e'd keep me job open.'

Buddy turned his head away so that his dad wouldn't see the tears that rolled on to his pillow.

'You keep on 'elping your mum wiv 'er exams – OK?' Buddy moved his head on the wet pillow. His dad laughed gently. 'Two flippin' geniuses in the family, that's all I need.'

There was a long pause. 'Hey, take care of 'er, though, won't you? Um? And yourself. I . . .'

He stood up and went to the door. Buddy brushed the tears away quickly and turned to look as the door swung open and the light fell full on his dad's face.

His dad glanced down and winked. 'It'll soon go,' he said and went out, closing the door behind him.

★

When Buddy got home from school, his mum was already back. She was sitting at the kitchen table and one look at her face told him that the news was bad. Her eyes were red and her mascara was smeared. She hadn't even taken off her coat.

She shrugged and tried to smile. 'Eighteen months,' she said and then shook her head as if she couldn't believe it.

Eighteen months. A year and a half.

Buddy put his school bag down and went and stood behind her. She raised her hand over her shoulder and he took hold of it and squeezed.

'They let me see him for a bit afterwards. He asked me if it would make any difference to the way I felt – if I'd change my mind about staying.' She turned round and Buddy could see the tears in her eyes. She bit her lip and then forced a smile. 'He reckons he'll only have to do fourteen months, maybe less. He was joking around – you know him.'

She let go of his hand and stood up. She walked down the hall, taking off her coat and laying it across the banisters, then went upstairs.

Buddy leaned against the sink and tried to imagine fourteen months. Fourteen months ago, he'd been thirteen and his mum had just left. It seemed an eternity. In fourteen months' time he would be nearly sixteen. All that time.

His mum came downstairs. Her eyes were brighter and this time she managed a real smile.

'Do you know what he said? Honestly, I'll never get used to that man. He said we had to make a cup of tea and listen to a Buddy Holly song. I ask you! He made me write down the name on a piece of paper so that I wouldn't forget it.'

Buddy made the tea and they went together into the front room. He looked at the paper and then went through the records until he found the right one. He slipped it on to the turntable and put the arm down carefully. The stylus crackled in the groove.

A plucked bass note, a tick-tock beat, then Buddy Holly's voice, high and hopeful, singing a message to them:

> 'Everyday,
> It's a-getting closer,
> Goin' faster than a roller coaster,
> Love like yours will surely come my way.'

# THE ORIGINALS
## Iconic • Outspoken • First

###  FOR THINKERS

- [ ] **Dear Nobody**
  *Berlie Doherty*

- [ ] **Buddy**
  *Nigel Hinton*

- [ ] **The Red Pony**
  *John Steinbeck*

- [ ] **The Wave**
  *Morton Rhue*

### ♡ FOR LOVERS

- [ ] **I Capture the Castle**
  *Dodie Smith*

- [ ] **Across the Barricades**
  *Joan Lingard*

- [ ] **The Twelfth Day of July**
  *Joan Lingard*

- [ ] **Postcards from No Man's Land**
  *Aidan Chambers*

### FOR REBELS

- [ ] **The Outsiders**
  *S. E. Hinton*

- [ ] **The Pearl**
  *John Steinbeck*

- [ ] **No Turning Back**
  *Beverley Naidoo*

### FOR SURVIVORS

- [ ] **Z for Zachariah**
  *Richard C. O'Brien*

- [ ] **After the First Death**
  *Robert Cormier*

- [ ] **Stone Cold**
  *Robert Swindells*

- [ ] **The Endless Steppe**
  *Esther Hautzig*

*What are you reading? Tell*  **@penguinplatform #OriginalYA**

YouTube

# 6 BOOKS TO MAKE YOU THINK

## ...AND CRY AND THINK AGAIN

### THE ORIGINALS

**DEAR NOBODY**
*by Berlie Doherty*

*Helen writes tender letters to her unplanned unborn baby.*

**THE RED PONY**
*by John Steinbeck*

*A celebration of a blessed but sometimes brutal adolescence in rural California.*

**BUDDY**
*by Nigel Hinton*

*Buddy's father has always lived on the edges of the criminal underworld, but things just got serious.*

**ALL THE BRIGHT PLACES**
*by Jennifer Niven*

*Violet is a girl who learns to live from a boy who wants to die.*

**THE ONE MEMORY OF FLORA BANKS**
*by Emily Barr*

*You always remember your first kiss – Flora remembers nothing else.*

**BOYS DON'T CRY**
*by Malorie Blackman*

*Dante Bridgeman didn't expect to be left holding the baby.*

*Thinkers follow:*     **#OriginalYA**